HOT VIKINGS - VOLUME 2

THE KING'S RAIDERS

PEYTON LAWSON

Edited by Rachael Lammie
Cover by Peyton Lawson

BEACHES AND TRAILS
PUBLISHING

ABOUT THE AUTHOR

Peyton Lawson writes Steamy Historical Viking Romance. Her edge-of-your-seat action and adventure stories feature strong, fearless characters who always get their HEA.
She enjoys reading and traveling.

For updates on book releases, book recommendations, Viking Trivia, Sales, and GIVEAWAYS, subscribe to her Newsletter!

www.peytonlawsonromance.com

- facebook.com/peytonlawsonromance
- x.com/plawson_romance
- instagram.com/beachesandtrailspublishing
- amazon.com/author/peytonlawsonromance
- bookbub.com/authors/peyton-lawson
- goodreads.com/peytonlawsonromance
- pinterest.com/beachesandtrailspublishing
- tiktok.com/@peytonlawsonbooks

ALSO BY PEYTON LAWSON

Ebooks and paperbacks

The Jürgensen Vikings

The King's Raiders

The Viking Settlers

Audiobooks

The Jürgensen Vikings

The King's Raiders

The Viking Settlers

THYRA

BEFRIENDED BY THE KING'S RAIDERS

PROLOGUE

THE WATERS HAD BEEN KIND. The ship sailed gently from Denmark with little fuss, and their journey would end by morning. Their destination was the Danish settlement on Scottish shores. Before they left, the King's Runemaster predicted a storm. The group was glad she had been wrong. The sky was clear, and a warm breeze travelled on the air.

While most Viking ships were simple, solid and sure, made for swift and easy travel and not made to be weighed down by unnecessary items. A ship sent by the King was made to be fearsome. The mere sight often rendered two responses: shock and awe or fear and dread. The King's ship was exceedingly vast, designed to carry his own personal forces and anything they collected from raids.

It was late evening. The sun had already begun to set, setting the horizon a fire with shades of orange and pink, signalling the following morning would be glorious. The rowers continued on steadily pushing the ship forward in the oceans waters while the rest of the men and women aboard either settled In for the night or sat playing games and drinking.

Out of earshot of the crew, at the prow stood six brave and fearsome warriors. They shared the same goal, a mission from the King. But even with their easy journey, frustrations and tempers ran high. They argued in hushed tones to keep their mission's true goal away from listening ears.

"Don't be foolish. We have information from one of the Jarl's men. It is clear, we should look to the south," argued the only woman in the group, Revna Antunson.

"I agree with Revna. We have the information from a sound source. So why ignore it and go on a wild goose chase?" Sven countered, giving his twin sister a nod of support.

Revna rolled her eyes. Her brother often backed her and always gave her a signalled nod of support. She didn't need it. She was the leader of the sword maidens and had bested him whilst sparing on multiple occasions. She appreciated his continued support, but at times like this, it felt patronising. It was always met with her customary eye roll.

"The Antunson's are right. What if while we follow other leads, someone else finds the treasure? The King will be displeased if we fail this mission," Toke Ketelsen said. Revna and Sven were both caught by surprise by Toke's support. He often sided with anyone other than Revna and fought hard against any and all of her ideas.

"I think we should head to the settlement and gather what we need before heading south. Our true mission need not be discovered if we make pleasantries," Sven said, glancing at Revna. Her arms were folded across her chest, clearly frustrated.

"No, we should change course now before it's too late, head to the point, and start looking there immediately. We can head to the settlement if we find nothing," Revna argued back.

The group squabbled between themselves to where voices began to raise. It was Leif who noticed first they were drawing unwanted attention. He cleared his throat and very significantly looked over his shoulder to a where several men sitting by the mast were arm wrestling. The group's arguing had caused them to forget their game and instead stop and stare.

"Enough!" Boomed Leif, now that he had their attention. "I am the commander here. I was tasked by the King to find the money the Jarl stole. I was tasked with finding it on these strange and wretched shores and returning it to him. I chose all of you because I believe there are no other Vikings I trust more or who are more capable of following orders." Leif kept his volume low, but his harsh tone emphasised his point, silencing them.

Sven exchanged a guilty glance with his sister, knowing that neither of them was entirely worthy of that trust.

"Did I make a mistake in choosing you all?" Leif asked after a significant pause. The group groaned, a couple muttering a half-hearted "No" in response.

"Then stop acting like bickering children straight off the breast and act like the warriors you are," Leif said, his tone becoming a shade warmer but no less commanding. "We have two very good options here. Let us settle this once and for all. A vote," Leif glanced at them each in turn. "Those in favour of changing course and heading south say, 'aye'."

Revna and Toke both spoke up immediately. Revna looked annoyed at her brother, who had sided with her moments before.

Sven grimaced. Lately, it seemed he could do no right by his sister.

"Those in favour of heading to the settlement first, say, 'Aye'," Leif continued.

Arne Wetsrip, Ullf Tranbarger and Sven Antunson said, "Aye" in unison. Leif Gastausen nodded his approval and turned to Sven.

"Whatever we choose to do, we must be smart about it. We can't draw suspicion," Arne cautioned.

"Sven is right. If we head to the settlement first, it will seem that we are only visiting on the King's wishes of good health and growth," Ulf seconded.

Leif nodded, satisfied. "Then the matter is settled. We continue our course to the Scottish settlement. From there, we dine, restock and head south from there. It shall look like just a regular visit by the King's men. Now fill your bellies, and rest up. We have a busy day ahead of us."

The group scattered, Arne and Ulf headed below deck to sleep, and Leif joined the group by the mast. Sven went to stand at the ship's prow, watching the sun's final descent over the horizon.

"You do not intend on informing the Jürgensens about the king's reward, do you?" Revna asked her brother as she came to stand next to him.

"Do you think me a fool, sister? Splitting the reward six ways is sharing enough. Our family needs that coin. Besides, once we have our share, we will no longer be restricted by the King's vessel. We can build a ship of our own. The world will be ours." Sven no longer saw the empty sea as he spoke, instead of imagining his own ship sailing on those open waters.

Revna nodded her approval. Her eyes glittered in the setting sun, making him wonder if she saw it too.

"We should thank them, really," Sven said with a mischievous grin.

Revna eyed him with annoyance and confusion. "And why is that?"

"If they had their wits about them, the Jarl would not have been able to steal from the Danegald. No treasure to find means no reward," Sven began.

Revna shook her head and turned to leave.

Sven's brow furrowed at the memory of all the Jarl's evil deeds. When he spoke, it was more to himself than to her. "Ignorant, pathetic fools, why should they get any reward? They let the Jarl commit such evil atrocities for far too long," Sven said, spitting his hatred overboard in this torrent of words.

"How will you keep the others from informing them? Arne and Ulf are two of the most honest men I have ever met. Toke is a fool who lets his mouth run away with him, and Leif takes his orders from the King," Revna asked as she scanned for listening ears.

Svan drew himself up. "You leave them to me, sister." He made the words a vow. "I take my mission seriously, but our family will always come first in my eyes."

CHAPTER 1

"Ship approaching!" yelled a voice from the docks informing the rest of the settlement that visitors had arrived. It was just after dawn, and the sun's rising colours framed the travelling ship in shades resembling fire, giving the large vessel an altogether fearsome appearance.

"Signal Sören and Ryker and the others," Thyra Bredahl said, sending the young man running into the settlement to inform the Jürgensens of the newcomers.

Thyra stood watching the ship from the far end of the dock. After the disaster that was the Jarl's visit, she stood at a distance, bow in hand, axe and sword on hip, ready for any fight that might come her way. As the vessel docked and the sun's rays no longer obscured the view, she could see the sails and flags attached blowing in the breeze. The King's colours? She threw her bow over her back and watched as several Vikings disembarked.

Five large Vikings stalked up the dock with pride, followed closely by a fellow sword maiden. The woman looked just as ferocious as the men. Thyra was a fellow sword maiden who appreciated the woman's evident strength. The men, on the other hand, didn't impress Thyra. She was just as skilled and strong as any of them and had several successful battles to her name.

Since none of this concerned her, she began to leave when one of the last of men disembarked, catching her eye. He was a rather tall specimen with long blond hair braided and tied back away from his face. His piercing blue eyes captured her attention as he looked her way.

His full lips framed with a small, well-kept beard creased into a slight polite grin. He inclined his head before continuing past her toward the remaining Jurgenson brothers. Thyra watched as Sören and Ryker spoke with the group before heading towards the council hut. Shaking herself out of her thoughts, her eyes fell from the blond man's strong bulking shoulders to his pert round buttocks and strong legs, proving she wasn't entirely immune to his charms. Somewhat put out, she headed to her hut, annoyed at herself for looking.

A few hours passed. The newcomer's arrival had nothing to do with her, and Thyra had spent her day wisely. She had restrung her bow, sharpened her blades and sparred with the younger sword maidens in training.

"Well done, Kaja. You are making great progress. You will make a fine sword maiden when your training is complete," Thyra said with a smile to one of the young women she was working with.

"Thyra," a voice came over her shoulder. Thyra turned to see Harold, one of the younger scouts hurrying toward her. "Sören summons you at once," he said, shifting from one foot to the next too impatient to be still as he waited for her to follow.

Thyra nodded and dismissed the young trainees for the day, then headed to the council hut with Harold.

On arrival, she found the group from earlier sitting in the hut accompanied by Ryker and
Sören. Discussions had clearly taken place and not gone well as everyone's faces were severe.

"What are my orders?" she asked, keeping her eyes on Sören.

"Our visitors here need to travel to the Point," Sören said, his eyes not leaving the group in front of him. "Thyra speaks several languages, including that of the locals. She is our best scout and one of our most skilled sword maidens. She is currently in the process of training our latest recruits. She shall act as your guide during your stay."

"With all due respect, Sören, I will not be babysitting our visitors. I will take them where they need to go, but I have important tasks to take care of here," Thyra said, hoping her protests wouldn't be disrespectful.

"Such as?" the female visitor asked with a playful smirk.

"Like Sören said, I am training our latest recruits," Thyra answered bluntly, turning toward Sören to see if he would agree or not.

"Are you expecting a battle presently? Are your forces not sufficient enough already?" the female visitor retorted.

Thyra could feel her temper flaring and clenched her fists tightly, happy that her sleeves were long enough to hide her anger. "I assure you our forces are well-equipped and the best warriors you have seen. That doesn't mean we should lack training. One can never be too prepared for battle," Thyra said with pride. She suppressed a small grin when her response seemed to silence the cocky visitor.

"Stop teasing, Revna," the blond Viking said playfully from where he leaned against the hut wall, near the back of the group.

"I will take them to the Point, but that is as far as I go," Thyra said, turning back to Sören.

"Your orders are unchanged. You will act as a guide," Sören countered calmly while his eyes raged at being challenged in front of guests.

"I will take them to the Point. We have other scouts who can accompany me and bring them back. My time is better spent with the recruits," Thyra insisted, not quite ready to back down.

"Do all your people speak to you with such disregard for your orders, or is it just the women?" one of the men asked, and a slight chuckle erupted from the group.

Sören drew himself up further if that were possible. The man's back was already straight. "Enough! Thyra, you will do as you are told or face the consequences of disobeying my orders!"

"I meant no disrespect Sören," Thyra said, bowing her head. The boom in Sören's voice brought back memories Thyra thought she had repressed, and once again, she was happy her sleeves hid her hands which had begun to tremble. "When do we leave?" She kept her eyes carefully on the floor as she asked, realizing she had gone too far.

"Dawn. You will spend the rest of your day preparing for the trip.

Our guests are welcome to rest after their journey and gather provisions. Tonight we feast to your safe arrival," Sören said.

"Sören," Thyra said, acknowledging the order. Swiftly she turned and left the hut, having no desire to stay and make small talk. As she approached the door, she happened to look up and caught the gaze of the handsome blond visitor who gazed at her with a sympathetic smile and a glint in his eye.

He stood and bowed, rushing ahead to open the door to the hut for her, a gesture that received an eye roll from Thyra, who was more than capable of opening a door for herself.

"I look forward to our journey together," he said as she walked through the door. "I am sure a woman like yourself is excellent at all she does."

She bit back an automatic retort, trying to ignore the hairs prickling at the back of her neck as his eyes scanned her face. After all, he had done nothing to earn such animosity from her.

He is charming. I will give him that....and a little too flattering, Thyra thought as she stormed past him, heading back to her trainees. He wants something. No man acts like that without a motive.

CHAPTER 2

Sven stood in the hut doorway and watched as Thyra stormed away, clearly irritated by her orders. There was something about the woman that called to Sven. If everything Sören had said about her was true, she was intelligent. Especially so if she was responsible for training the recruits. She was obviously a skilled warrior. She would be difficult to hide things from, which worried him. He was afraid she would notice things he would rather stay hidden about their mission.

All the same, Sven couldn't help but feel for her when Sören chastised her in front of the group, and it annoyed him how Revna taunted her. A part of him wanted to check she was alright. He debated this feeling as he watched her walk away. He took off after her, thinking she might make a better ally than an enemy.

"Thyra, a moment of your time, please," he said as he caught up with her.

She stopped and turned to face him…reluctantly. Sven could tell this much from the groan that left her lips.

"What? Do you think I maybe do not have enough to do? Especially now that I am to spend the next few days babysitting you and your friends?" she shot back.

"I understand your frustrations, and your time is indeed valuable. But may I ask why you are so irritated by the expedition? Is it purely because of who we are? My friends and sister were sent here on this mission by our King. And while I apologise on their behalf, I also acknowledge they can be difficult at times." He paused significantly. "Or is the trail to the point so dangerous?" Sven asked, with a sly smile tugging at his lips.

Thyra's looked up at him and her face creased in anger; she huffed out a puff of air and turned to storm off once more. Sven's long legs had no trouble keeping pace with her.

"Of course not. It's a tedious and simple expedition," Thyra said suddenly, whirling to face him. "A child could find it. *My* time is better spent on more important things. Moreover, it is but a few days away by sea. It would be much easier for you all to board your ship and sail there. The waters are calm, and despite the underwater rocks, our boats have sailed through with ease on multiple occasions." She turned and headed back to the sword maidens' village with that.

Sven could not help but pause to enjoy the sight of her. Her anger put a pleasant flush to her cheeks. The setting sun gave highlights to her hair that brought out copper highlights in the brown. She was mighty to behold, passionate and strong.

He raced after her and caught her arm. "You are right we could sail there, but we have been on the sea for so long it is nice to feel the ground beneath my feet once more," Sven said, making a sweeping gesture to indicate the dirt under his feet.

"You are a Viking, are you not? Sailing is in your blood," Thyra shot back, finally stopping abruptly and facing Sven. Her face no longer held anger but an obnoxious teasing grin.

"Or perhaps you are frightened like a child, and that is why you cut your journey short and stopped here," she said, folding her arms over her chest and scanning Sven up and down, sizing him up. "The mothers do tell such compelling stories of Selkies and sea monsters. Perhaps your mother's tales still frighten you?"

Sven couldn't help himself. He couldn't contain his laughter any longer. Much as he admired this woman's resolve and wit, this statement was too much. He burst out laughing, holding his ribs with one hand to ease the stitch in his side.

When he looked back up at her, she seemed surprised by his

outburst. She had meant her words as an insult, but Sven had taken no offence. If anything, her reaction made him admire the woman more.

"Perhaps you are a selkie yourself," he said, finally straightening up and wiping a stray tear from his eye.

"I beg your pardon?" she asked, drawing back and crossing her arms as she stared him down.

"Selkies are bewitching creatures famed for their beauty and ability to lure a man to his death at sea. I think you match that description. You a so bewitching I haven't been able to leave your side since first eyeing you. I think you do not know how beautiful you are with your pale skin, dark eyes and dark hair," Sven said. To his surprise, he meant every word. Sven had always been a flirt and a charmer and was never short of female admirers.

Sven watched as Thyra eyed him uncertainly, flustered by his sudden interest. From her reaction, Sven could tell she wasn't used to having any kind of male attention. If that was the case, Sven wondered why. She was a beautiful woman, strong and tall for a woman, but not so tall that he didn't tower over her in the way he liked. Sven had no doubt that Thyra could handle herself, and the thought that she could most likely knock him on his backside only made Sven admire her more.

Yet she wasn't what he normally found attractive in a woman. He liked his women to be short, small enough to tuck under his arm that he could act as mighty protector. This woman hardly needed his help. If anything, she looked as though she could handle a sword better than him.

She seemed to have come to the same conclusion. "Get your group ready by dawn. The sooner we leave, the sooner I can be done with you," she snapped before storming off.

Sven stood grinning, watching her march away and teased her by offering a playful wave when she glanced back. He chuckled when she realised he was watching, and she broke out into a slight jog to get away faster.

She might not have been his type, but Sven had never looked forward to an expedition more than he was this one.

CHAPTER 3

THYRA WOKE THE FOLLOWING DAY, determined not to let the visitors get the better of her. She had been embarrassed enough the day prior. Thyra instead focused on how she could find some good on this trip. For starters, the trip to the Point could restock needed supplies. The healer required herbs and Thyra knew where to forage for them. There were many places along the trail where plants grew in abundance.

At least the weather was calm enough. A soft breeze danced and tugged at her hair, and the sun shone beautifully without it being overly hot. She dressed accordingly but packed warmer clothes in case of a change in weather. Since arriving on these strange shores, Thyra had discovered how easily the weather could change.

She packed her weapons and a pouch for her herbs and left to gather her horse. Sören had told her to meet the visitors at the edge of the settlement fairly early in the morning, and she was ready in plenty of time. So it was. Thyra was surprised to find the female of the group angrily pounding towards her the moment she left her home.

"Is there a problem?" Thyra asked, looking askance at the young woman.

"We leave soon, and your sword maidens are not ready. My maidens would never be so lazy," she spat.

Thyra felt her temper flaring. The woman seemed to have taken a dislike to her. Thyra, though she'd tried to keep an open mind, had found the feeling mutual when the meeting with Sören and Ryker had ended. This attack wasn't helping any to revise this opinion. Thyra prided herself on training the best sword maidens, and they had more than proven their worth in the battle against the army Lord Beacham had gathered not long ago. In anticipation of any retaliation, the Jürgensen brothers had increased training for both the sword maidens and the men. They had become a force to be reckoned with.

"Watch your tongue, or I will rip it from your mouth. My sword maidens are anything but lazy. They fought off an army not long ago, and right after, they increased their training and have proven themselves against some of our best male fighters while sparring. They are resting. Leave them be. We do not need them for the trip to the Point," Thyra snapped, squaring up to Revna.

"Warriors do not need rest. They are not heading into battle. They are accompanying us on an expedition," Revna snapped back.

"Do you have such low confidence in your fighting skills that you need my forces to protect you on a child's errand?" Thyra asked with a grin.

Their shouting had alerted the sword maidens, who all stood at their doors watching. Several cheered at Thyra's retort.

"You think to mock me?" Revna snarled through gritted teeth.

"I do not mock you. You mock yourself," Thyra answered.

Revna and Thyra stood practically nose to nose, sizing each other up, just as stubborn as the other.

"The sword maidens stay here, do not worry. I am warrior enough to protect you if anything should happen," Thyra said, knocking Revna aside as she brushed past her and headed for her horse.

To make matters worse, Sören and Ryker stood with the group at the settlement gates waiting for Thyra.

"Thyra, glad to see you are in better spirits today," Ryker joked, receiving a sharp look of disapproval from Sören.

"Indeed I am. At first, I may not have been happy with my orders, but I am a woman of honour, and I respect Sören's decision. Also, our healer needs more herbs, so I have my own tasks to accomplish on this trip," Thyra answered.

This seemed to satisfy the waiting men. The large, grim-faced

Viking who'd done most of the speaking yesterday gave a sharp approval at her words. "Thank you for guiding us, Thyra. Allow me to introduce myself and my comrades properly," he said, with a sharp look at the others.

By his clothes and how he commanded himself, it was apparent to Thyra that he was the group leader.

"I am Leif Gustausen, leader of this group. I believe you have already met Sven and Revna Antunsen," he gestured towards the blond and his twin sister.

Sven, it's nice to finally have a name to the face, Thyra thought. She nodded towards Leif and Sven and gave Revna a dismissive look.

"Sven is my second. Here we have Toke Ketelsen, Ulf Tranbarger, and last but not least, we have Arne Westrup," Leif continued. Each group member, except for Revna, nodded at the introduction of their name.

"With all due respect Leif, I know you are the group leader, but I am the leader on this expedition. While the trail to the point is not overly dangerous, I know these lands better than most, and there are still many ways to get lost. I do not have to tell you of the love lost between Vikings and the Kelts," Thyra said, drawing herself up and hoping she was making her point clear.

"As you wish," Leif said, giving a warning look at the rest of the group, who nodded their understanding.

They set out with Thyra taking the lead, the rest following closely behind. The point was easily a two or three days ride depending on the weather, so they needed to find somewhere to set up camp for the night. Thyra knew the perfect spot, a clearing in a thicket of trees south past the hills leading into the valley.

They rode for hours with the visitors chatting amongst themselves behind her. Thyra was glad no one chose to speak with her. She had nothing of interest or importance she wished to say to any of them, and she feared she might lose her temper if she was forced to speak with Revna again.

They travelled over the hills and towards the valley, following a small stream through the trees. There was a quicker way to the point, but with Thyra not knowing much of the visitors, she didn't want to risk taking them through the villages. She spoke the locals' language, had often negotiated trades with them, and had recovered the shaky relationship between several small towns and the settlement. But, for all she knew, these new visitors could end all that, so she was happy to take them the long way through the woods. Besides, they were Vikings. They hardly needed to be coddled in comfort at the local inn. One night sleeping under the stars would not hurt them any.

The sun sank lower in the sky, taking a lot of the light from within the trees. The wind had picked up, and soft grey clouds rolled in. Thyra could see the dark clouds in the distance. Another day or two and a storm would surely be upon them. Hopefully, they would reach the point before then.

Thankfully they reached the clearing she'd had in mind before the light failed entirely. "Halt," Thyra said, stopping her horse and dismounting. "we set up camp here and continue on in the morning." She pulled her pouch from one of her saddlebags and tied her horse to a small tree.

"Scared of travelling the woods in the dark?" Revna teased, but Thyra didn't rise to it.

"By all means, if you wish to travel these woods after dark, be my guest. Good luck navigating the cliffs just past those hills. I'd hate to see that pretty face of your splattered across the ravine," Thyra said. Her retort caused Sven and Arne to chuckle. Revna growled and dismounted, stalking off towards the stream for some water.

Sven dismounted, but to Thyra's surprise, he ignored his sister entirely and instead came to bother her. Great. He was probably about to tell her to back off and quit sparring with his sister. Thyra was in no mood or frame of mind to talk to him, so she walked past him, ignoring him entirely, instead of heading straight towards Leif and the rest of the group.

"Feel free to start a fire. It gets cold in the forest after sunset. If one of you wants to hunt for supper, I suggest heading east up the hill. There is normally plenty of small game in those rocks. Sometimes a deer or two if you go into the thicket just beyond," she said. She headed in the other direction entirely with a wave, making for the trees below camp.

"Where are you going?" Arne asked after her,

She answered over her shoulder without pausing. "I'm going to hunt for herbs. I will be back shortly."

Thyra travelled a little up the hill deeper into the woods. If she turned back, she could still make out the camp through the trees, and their voices were distant enough for her to have some space to think, but not too distant where she wouldn't hear if anything should occur.

She collected mugwort and thyme, then headed down towards the stream a short distance ahead of camp for some yarrow. Then, with her pouches almost full, she found another clearing in the trees to collect the last thing on her list. So she knelt by the trees gathering lingonberries when she heard rustling and the snapping of twigs underfoot.

"I'm surprised a warrior like yourself knows herblore," Sven's deep voice said from behind her.

Thyra didn't bother to turn to look in his way. She kept herself busy with her task until her bag was full. Only then did she speak.

"My mother was a healer. So I was versed in herblore before I could pick up a sword or bow," she informed him when it was clear he wasn't leaving.

"How nice to learn such a useful skill from your mother. Did you learn to fight from your father then?" Sven asked, taking a seat on a fallen tree stump.

Thyra didn't like discussing her father. She had nothing but fearful and disturbing memories of the man who was more a monster than anything from her mother's tales. Her memory flashed to her, hiding in caves, holes and any place dark and small enough she could fit into whenever he was in a temper. Her father had never married her mother and purely only stuck around to have something to yell at and hit when the other men taunted him for his lack of fighting skills. Then, as a show of force and reinforcing his so-called skills, he would come home from the tavern drunk and take his anger out on Thyra and her mother.

The man had been a coward and a beast. Thyra's dreams were still haunted by the memories of the brute. He was why she became a sword maiden. She had learned to fight purely, so she was skilled enough to protect herself and her mother. Once she was skilled and strong enough, she'd taken her anger out on him to give him a taste of what it felt like to be afraid.

He never returned after that.

"I do not have a father," she answered eventually, after realising she had been lost in thought for too long. She could see Sven was about to question further and immediately changed the subject.

"Revna is your sister? It must be nice having a sibling, especially one you seem quite close to as you travel together."

Sven looked started about the sudden shift in conversation. He eyed her sharply but softened when he saw...something. She had no idea what...in her eyes.

"She is. Though she can be a handful sometimes," he said with a wry chuckle. "What about you?"

"Unfortunately, I was not so fortunate. I was my mother's only child," Thyra said, tucking the last herbs she'd collected into her bag and flinging it over her shoulder. "Do you have no other family?"

"While I am close with Revna, she is not my only sibling. We are the oldest of eight. They are home with our parents," Sven said, his face changing from happy to sad at the mention of his family. "I miss them dearly when we are away. My family are everything to me," he finished.

"It's nice to see. I will admit, it's a rare quality these days," Thyra said.

Sven looked up at her and smiled back. They looked on at each other for a few moments, comfortable in their silence and comfortable enough with each other that nothing needed to be said.

It was...nicer than she expected.

"Your eyes are quite striking," Thyra breathed after a moment.

"Thank you, they are my mother's. I should probably give them back," Sven said with a wicked grin that made her laugh.

Their moment was interrupted when Revna burst through the trees. She looked positively furious to find her brother standing with Thyra. Wordlessly, she grabbed Sven's collar and dragged him back towards camp.

Startled, Thyra stared blankly after her, watching in amusement as Sven struggled against his sister's grasp. His protests grew fainter as

Revna cursed him out back through the trees. Shaking her head, Thyra headed back to camp at a much slower pace, allowing the twins to work out their differences without her around.

What an interesting family...I wonder why they're really here.

As she emerged from the trees, she glanced over to the horses who grazed peacefully and saw Sven and Revna in deep conversation. Revna's face was ablaze with frustration. Thyra tucked her herbs into the saddlebags and settled on a log by the fire Leif had made. She fussed with the flames, adding another stick to the blaze. However, it hardly needed it while listening intently to the conversation behind her.

"Why were you following anyway, Revna? I am not a child, and I don't consider being treated as such," Sven's voice boomed.

Well, so much for being discreet. The entire group had looked over to watch the exchange between the siblings. Thyra glanced at the others and settled in to watch with them, enjoying the night's entertainment as it unfolded.

"If you didn't act like one, I wouldn't treat you like one. So keep your mind on the mission and out of your trousers," Revna snapped back.

The group, Thyra included, stifled a grin and a few chuckles escaped lips. Thyra gave Sven a sideling look and saw his cheeks were flushed red.

Unfortunately, the chuckles alerted brother and sister that they were being watched. Thyra glanced again at the others as Sven dragged Revna further away out of earshot as they continued to argue. Tempers flared when Revna struck out and slapped her brother; the sound echoed through the clearing.

This was the last straw for Toke, who sat next to Leif, skinning the rabbits they had snared. He stood up and yelled loud enough for Revna to hear. "I think it is you who acts like a spoilt child Revna. We are not too far from the settlement. Perhaps we should send you back. Maybe you are overtired from our travels and should rest with the other sword maidens," He tossed his freshly skinned rabbit to Ulf, who shoved a stick through it and mounted it with the others over the fire.

"I fight just as well as any of you. If something should happen on this trip, you, of all people, will need my help. I refuse to be left behind," Revna yelled, storming over and clapping Toke hard around the head.

Toke jumped to his feet and squared up to Revna, who didn't back down despite the large man towering over her and the knife he wielded through his hand still dripped in blood from his grisly task.

"Don't waste your breath, my friend. We can send her home all we want. She will just follow anyway. Pay her no mind. Her issue is with me. Sibling rivalry as it were," Sven said, nudging his sister with his shoulder as he walked past to join the rest of the group at the fire.

Thyra watched Sven closely for the rest of the evening. After his argument with Revna – which Thyra had quickly deduced was about her – he'd refused to meet her gaze and kept busy tending to the horses or sharpening his blades. Thyra watched how he was with his sister until they retired for the night. She remembered how sad he had become thinking of his family back home in Denmark and realised that he loved his twin deep down, even if they didn't always get along.

Perhaps I have misjudged him. His words seem genuine enough. I have no doubt Revna can take care of herself, but that doesn't stop him from protecting her, Thyra thought.

As the night deepened and the moon chased the clouds for an hour before disappearing behind them completely, everyone settled down for the night. Thyra tried to find any excuse to converse with Sven. Still, he always seemed busy with tedious tasks or found any reason to sit alone away from the group. It stung a little how he suddenly began to avoid her, and Thyra had trouble explaining why his actions hurt so much.

A harsh wind pushed through the trees, and thunder rumbled far in the distance. She suddenly didn't have time to think or worry about Sven and his sister. Instead, she needed to keep her mind on her task. If a storm threatened, it would cause them to change their path, elongating the journey by a day at least. Finally, Thyra fell into a fitful sleep, working out several other paths they could take to the point, all of them designed to keep the journey short and safe in the wake of the storm.

CHAPTER 4

THYRA DIDN'T GET much sleep that night. The makeshift shelters Leif and his men had made were far too small for Thyra's liking, and she didn't much appreciate being forced to share what little space she had with Revna. The winds howling through the trees caused the shelters to shake and leak. The rain splattering across Thyra's face didn't help things either. When she did try to sleep, her mind flashed with memories from her past. The thunder reminded her of her father's booming voice and pounding footsteps, the sound of chairs crashing against the walls as he tore their home apart looking for her. Finally, she removed herself from the shelter and settled under the trees. It wasn't much more comfortable but gave her the much-needed room to stretch and breathe.

The storm had calmed somewhat when Thyra woke from what little sleep she had managed to get. She stretched and headed back towards the middle of their camp to find Revna and Sven trying to relight the fire with damp wood.

"Sleep well?" Ulf asked as Thyra approached,

Revna snorted when she heard the question. "I think not. Apparently, our guide here is too good to sleep in our shelters. Or perhaps you just didn't want to share a space with me after our encounter yesterday," Revna said. She tried to taunt Thyra into a rebuttal again, but her tone betrayed her. Thyra almost detected, what? Concern?

Perhaps the woman wasn't as hard and cruel as she initially seemed.

"Worry not, Revna, you occupy little of my thoughts to warrant concern," Thyra said, rubbing her tired face with her palms.

"She means no harm. If she isn't teasing, taunting or arguing with you, that's when you need to be concerned. My sister has a strange way of showing her affections," Sven said, sitting next to Thyra and handing her some bread and cheese he pulled from his bag.

Thyra accepted it happily.

"Is the trail still safe after the storm?" Revna asked, handing Thyra her water pouch.

"There is a shallow part of the river just beyond the trees. We should be able to cross there and take a shortcut around the caves at the bottom of the hill," Thyra said, accepting the water pouch and washing down the dry bread and cheese.

"I knew our guide would not let us down. Sören did indeed send his best with us," Sven said. Revna rolled her eyes and walked away to check her horse, while Thyra ignored his comment altogether, unsure how to react.

The group waited patiently for the rest of the rain to stop and for Toke to finally wake. Sven hovered, always at Thyra's side, finding any excuse to flirt with Thyra and was making an effort to be extra kind. Thyra thought it was his way of apologising for avoiding her the night before. Still, she kept her head clear of thoughts that might have proved distracting by instead thinking about the expedition at hand.

When Toke was taking too long to wake, and the group grew impatient, Revna splashed his face with water rousing him with a start. Once the group was fed and properly attired to brave the elements, Thyra led the group past the clearing and further down the hills to where the stream stopped. The sound of the river waters rushing and crashing against the shore told them they were headed in the right direction. But unfortunately, they didn't get far before they were forced to stop. The section of the river they needed to cross had been flooded; the overnight storm had washed away the makeshift bridge.

"We can't cross here. It's far too dangerous now. The horses won't make it across," Thyra said, scanning the area for another break in the river for them to cross.

"Shall we head back and find a different route?" asked Toke with a yawn.

"No, if we go back, we will just be slowing our journey down," Thyra answered.

"There are other sections of river we should be able to cross. The bulk of the flood is here," Leif said to which Thyra agreed.

"Arne, Toke, head upriver and search for a crossing. Revna and Ulf head up the hill and search for another route," Leif instructed and the group split.

"Revna, Ulf, be careful. The trail up that hill often has mudslides when it rains, don't force the horses to make the trip. If there is the smallest doubt in your mind, head back. If needed, we can find other ways," Thyra said, receiving a nod in thanks from the pair before they ushered their horses into a canter up the hill.

"Let us head downstream. Perhaps the river will show us another way," Leif said. He turned quickly and headed downstream, leaving Sven and Thyra enough space to chat amongst themselves privately.

"He is....intense. Is he always like this? So serious?" Thyra asked,

"He is a man on a mission. He needs to succeed. He wants the King to think well of him. He may be considered for a higher position if he does well," Sven answered.

"It is not easy to be so ambitious," Thyra said, and Sven nodded.

"Well spoken! In truth, I am fairly curious about you, for you seem to not be ambitious at all." Sven said.

Thyra wondered if he felt he could speak more freely as Leif had travelled far enough ahead to still be in sight but far enough to leave them alone. "Curious how?" Thyra asked as she lifted a branch with one hand, holding it aloft that he might ride under without ducking.

"You took this expedition without asking our mission," Sven answered,

"I take my orders from Sören. My orders were to be your guide. I have no reason to know why," She answered honestly. She was so annoyed in being ordered to babysit that she never thought to ask, and now she frankly didn't really care. "Does blind obedience seem to be without ambition?" Her lips quirked into a smile. "Perhaps I am more so because I know doing what one is told also has its benefits when being considered for a higher position."

"Perhaps I have not given you enough credit. I have underestimated you, perhaps?" Sven asked, and Thyra blushed.

"Why are you here?" she asked, changing the subject as his tone was becoming more than a little flirtatious, and she wasn't sure exactly how she felt about that.

"You are aware of the troubles with the Jarl Halfden?" Sven asked to which Thyra nodded her reply.

"He stole treasure from the Danegeld. We are tasked to retrieve it. We have it on good authority that the Jarl left it at the point," Sven informed her.

Thyra frowned. If the King had ordered such a mission and had not asked for the Jürgensens' assistance, there could be a valid reason to distrust them. "Why are you telling me this?" she asked, wondering if she was even supposed to be privy to this information.

"Your time is valuable, and I wanted you to know you are not wasting this time helping us," Sven shrugged.

Thyra appreciated his honesty but was still uneasy about having information clearly not meant for her. She told herself she did not care why they had been ordered on this mission. It was none of her business. Her job was to deliver these Vikings to where they needed to go. In the meantime, she could enjoy Sven's company as much as she liked. It helped that he was pleasant to look at.

Sven leant down off his horse and pulled at a passing bush. Once straightened, he squared his shoulders and cleared his throat. "A flower for the lady, as thanks for lending us your precious time and attention," Sven said, presenting Thyra with a white petaled flower with yellow and red at its centre.

Thyra hid a smile. "Thank you, but I feel your words are lost when you offer me a poisonous flower."

Sven threw it down like a burning flame and vigorously whipped his hand on his clothes, pulling out his water pouch and pouring its condense over his hands. Seeing such a man rendered full of fear over a small delicate flower made Thyra laugh uproariously.

Sven watched her laugh as he dried off his hands before breaking into laughter himself. Then, the laughter died down, and the pair stared at each other, allowing their horses to be their eyes, trusting them to carry their riders safely where they needed to go.

"You have a wonderful laugh. I would like to hear it more," Sven said, his voice breathy and seductive.

"Your eyes twinkle when you smile," Thyra said with a wink.

She surprised herself by returning his flirtations but liked the feel of her hands growing sweaty and her pulse racing. These were all sensations new to her and exciting to explore.

"You truly are remarkable, Thyra," Sven said, nudging his horse closer to hers to the point their legs were almost crushed between the two giant beasts.

Sven licked his lips and slowly began to lean towards her. To her surprise, Thyra followed suit. She could smell his breath, and her eyes were locked on his bottom lip.

"My dear Thyra, if I was a gambling man, I would say you want me to kiss you," Sven teased,

"Then take the bet," Thyra answered.

Just as their lips were about to touch, Leif yelled in the distance. Both riders pulled away, looking forward only to realise Leif was further ahead than they thought, for he was no longer in sight. They spurred their horses onwards with a frustrated glance at one another, racing through the trees.

CHAPTER 5

LEIF STOOD in a clearing of what appeared to be the abandoned remains of a camp. Makeshift shelters, some still erect, some knocked down by the winds, made a semi-circle around a fire long extinguished. Other remains showed the camp had been left behind in a hurry.

Thyra stood astonished at what she saw. She had travelled this path plenty of times. How had she not noticed a camp before? Had Jarl Halfden stayed there when fleeing the Jurgenson brothers? How long had the camp lain empty?

Sven and Leif rummaged through the remains, turning over blankets and flags, brandishing the Jarl's sigil and broken weapons, a mix of spears, bows and axes. Had a battle taken place before Halfden fled?

"Look here," Leif said, picking up a broken chest, its lid barely clinging to its last hinge. It looked like it had been prized open and trampled on.

Sven barged past Thyra, almost knocking her over and lunged at the chest, yanking it hard from the weeds entangled with the remains. He yelled when he realised the interior was empty and tossed the chest hard against a nearby tree, shattering what remained of the heavy box.

Thyra only just managed to hide her feelings from playing out on her face. Sven's outburst shocked her. The way he lunged at the chest as if his life had depended on its discovery. That's when the realisation hit her like a wave. All the pleasantries, all the flirtations, had been a lie. A way to keep her sweet so she would help him reach his goal. She felt foolish, used, betrayed, and anger raced through her. She turned to look away, not wanting Sven to catch her eye as she raged internally.

"Let's keep looking," Leif said, and Thyra could hear the pair tearing the remains of the camp apart with newfound energy and frustration. They appeared to have forgotten she was there at all.

Thyra wandered to the edge of the camp, wanting space away from Sven when she noticed a notch in a tree. If you were not looking for it, you could easily miss it. It had been placed strategically to hide another path.

This path leads to the caves at the bottom of the valley. Surely, Halfden and his men wouldn't go there. They are known for flooding. But then Halfden wouldn't know these lands like I do, She thought, raising her hand to the notch in the tree, trying to determine from the wear upon the edges how long ago it might have been made. She wasn't sure. The mark wasn't fresh, but it hadn't been softened by the elements too deeply yet. A few months? Half a year?

Thyra debated telling Leif and Sven. She hesitated momentarily, overtaken by her feelings of anger towards him and thinking if Halfden escaping to the caves was a real possibility. But, unfortunately, she didn't have much time to consider these things before she heard footsteps approaching. She turned to see Sven eyeing her suspiciously. His face was no longer the face of beauty and kindness she had witnessed. Instead, he stood a man red in the face, angry, with his hands clenched into tight fists with white knuckles. His face reminded Thyra of her father, apart from the blue eyes and blond hair.

"What are you hiding?" he demanded through gritted teeth as he shoved her hard to one side to see what she had been looking at.

CHAPTER 6

THYRA STUMBLED BUT, with some effort, quickly managed to stay on her feet. She turned back to face Sven, rage swimming in her blood. How dare he lay his hands on her like that! His hand went to the small axe tucked into her belt. She wanted to swing it at him and make him see his mistake.

Sven ignored her completely. He stood looking at the notch, then walked through the trees a short distance before instantly storming, his eyes blazing as he charged at Thyra. She stood her ground, not letting him see an ounce of regret or fear, instead of letting her anger mirror his.

"Traitor," he spat at her, low enough for Leif not to hear.

"I am no such thing!" she snapped back, her hand tightening on her axe. "You should watch how you talk to me. And if you ever lay a hand on me again, I will remove said hand myself," she raged, shoving him hard in the shoulder with the handle of her axe.

"You saw this path. If I had not noticed, you would have kept it hidden. You had no intentions of following Sören's orders or helping us," he roared.

His shout alerted Leif to the situation, who looked up at them both with a frown.

"I made a mistake trusting you, telling you of our quest. I will not be so foolish again!" Sven boomed, his voice startling birds out of the trees.

"What is going on over here?" Leif asked, wiping his hands on his pants to knock off the dirt as he walked over.

"There is another path leading out of the camp. One *she*," he pointed an accusing finger at Thyra, "intended to keep it to herself. Why? To track down the treasure yourself later? Instead, I should drag you in front of the King myself and let you accept the same fate as others who steal from him," Sven roared.

Thyra stepped back, hurt by his cruel words. Anger swallowed the hurt, using it to fuel her arm as she swung her axe at him, forcing him to jump back to avoid being hit. Roaring now, she charged at him again, shoving him hard in the shoulder, causing him to smack him back into the notched tree.

"You are crazy. You do not know me, do not think you do! If you did, you would know how truly wrong you are. I hesitated, yes, that is true, but not for the reasons you think. You have reliable information from one of the Jarl's men about the treasure's whereabouts. That is why I was instructed to guide you to the Point. That is where I intend to take you. This path and this camp are just as new to me as you," she yelled, stepping so close their faces almost touched.

"All the more reason to tell us about your discovery!" Sven boomed as the rest of the group rode into camp.

"It felt like a wild goose chase. The camp has long since been abandoned. The chest you found is empty. For all we know, they camped here and left for the Point, which is where your information takes you," Thyra screamed back.

Leif gently placed a hand on Thyras's shoulder and pulled her slowly away from Sven.

"Enough bickering like children," he said, ending the argument. "Where does the path lead?"

He had asked Thyra calmly, even kindly. Thyra glared at Sven, slowly pulling her gaze away to look up at Leif, reining in her anger enough to answer him clearly.

"Nowhere of note. At the bottom of the hill are a small gathering of caves. They lead nowhere. It's a dead end. Be my guest and look if you don't believe me. I was instructed to guide you to the Point and nowhere else, so if you choose to go; you go alone," Thyra said, her anger slowly dissipating. After all, her anger wasn't towards Leif.

Unfortunately, Thyra knew the caves all too well and had no intention of going inside them ever again. She had sheltered there once in a particularly bad storm, which was how she knew they flooded. But even more so, she hated the dark and especially enclosed spaces. It was far too easy to get lost in the caves, and she didn't fancy being stuck inside one of them. Especially given the way she found it hard to breathe when she neared those dark and awful places. She would not lose herself to fear and panic in front of these men, especially Revna, who already showed disdain for her.

"Then leave," Sven said in the harshest tone Thyra had heard thus far. She swore hatred blazed across his face as he walked past her and mounted his horse.

Thyra stood in the remains of the camp and watched the group ride through the trees without her. She waited until they were out of sight before she left. Anger still raced in her blood as she mounted her steed and kicked at its ribs harder than she intended, instantly regretting her actions against the poor horse.

Forget about them, Thyra. Leave them to their goose chase. It's none of your concern what they do, she thought as she rode off back towards the settlement.

CHAPTER 7

THE STORM THYRA thought had passed seemed to wake up once more as she left the camp. The further she rode, the heavier the rain began to fall, worsening with each passing minute. After only a short distance, she pulled her horse to a halt and looked at the sky. It had been bright and sunny moments earlier, and now the sky was roiling with black clouds. Lightning flashing within, trying to break free. She glanced back over her shoulder, considering what she knew of the caves.

The hills above acted as cover during the sunny days. Still, a runoff caused the caves to become tortuous and flood, cutting off some passages entirely from the outside. A man could easily drown in such a place.

They are Vikings. I know Sven may be stupid, but surely there is enough of them to look out for one another. Besides, she thought at least one would have mind enough to know not to venture into wet caves.

But Thyra was a woman of her word and a woman of honour, and while her anger made her want to leave them to their fate, her conscience wouldn't let her. It was sunny when they descended the hill. Once inside, they will not know of the rain, and they don't know the twists of the caverns, she thought.

"Empathy will be my death," she said to her horse, turning it around and riding back at full speed.

Thyra's horse struggled to stay standing as his hooves sank into the wet ground and made their way towards toe caves. Thunder roared through the sky, and lightning flashed as rain pounded in waves rivalled the seas. Arne stood at the mouth of the caves, visibly struggling with something. He ran to Thyra as she jumped from her horse.

"They aren't answering; I have called for them several times since the storm began. I think they have gone too deep. I fear for them. What shall we do?" He asked, raising his voice to be heard over the rushing water that rolled over the hill, hiding the cave's mouth like a waterfall.

"Head west, you will find a small town, tell them of your friends trapped in the cave, bring as many men as you can," Thyra roared over the crashing water from the hilltop. "They will know how to rescue them."

"I don't speak the language," Arne responded,

"They speak several languages in that town. You will find someone to help. Now go, I will head inside and search for them but hurry," Thyra insisted, pushing Arne towards the horses, which grew agitated as the thunder boomed around them.

Due to her fear, Thyra had not ventured far inside the caves, but she had heard plenty about the twisting passages and where some of them might lead. She took several deep breaths, gathering herself before she rushed inside past the waterfall now engulfing the mouth of the cave. The cold, dirty water crashed down on her as she ran inside. She shivered and found a log and some stone; she smashed the rocks together and lit a small torch to help her see, hoping it would eliminate her fears. It did not. Her hands trembled, and her chest grew tight with every step she took.

'Where are you, child?' Her father's voice rang in her ears, 'Either you come out, or I will beat your mother twice, once for her and once for you,'

She leaned back against the wet moss-covered cave wall squeezing her eyes shut. Stop it, stop it, stop it, it's not real, he isn't here. She took in a shaky breath and carried on, crouching as the roof dipped low in one passage.

'Papa no, please,' her memory flashed as her father found her and grabbed at her arm, yanking her from her hiding spot so hard he'd dislocated her shoulder.

It's not real; you are not that scared child anymore; you are a brave warrior who has taken down men twice your size. Breathe Thyra, Breathe. She reminded herself, standing up as the passage opened in front of her. She marched forward, each step a triumph of courage.

"Sven? Revna? Leif?"

No one replied.

She strode forward, calling down passage after passage, trying to discover which path to take. Sven needed her. It was partly her fault for leaving them to take this path alone. Guilt stabbed at her. She would never forgive herself if they were hurt because of her foolish fears.

The torch she lit offered little light in the darkness of the caves, and its light shook as she tried to fight her fear and the cold.

With so little light to guide her, she didn't see the depression on the floor until it was too late. Thyra cried out as she twisted her ankle. Quickly she struggled upright again, hardly noticing the pain as she had felt worse. But as she regained her footing, she slipped and dropped her torch. It splashed into a puddle and extinguished, leaving Thyra panting for breath in complete and utter darkness.

Fear took over her heart as memories from her childhood flooded back. She was trapped in the dark alone, with no way out and the storm threatening a flood outside.

"Sven!" she screamed out of reflex rather than fear. Her scream echoed long and loud through the cave. It was a cry of pure and utter helplessness and fear. The terror in her own voice was enough to make her blood grow cold.

No response came. She was alone, miles underground, where no one would ever find her.

CHAPTER 8

THE CAVES HELD SO many passages that the group split up to cover more ground after they entered. Sven knew caves. He had explored many such places before, so he marked his way with a soft rock acting as chalk to save losing his path. Later he knew he would be thankful he had done so.

When Sven heard Thyra's voice echoing through the cave, the first thing he noticed was the alarm in her voice. He turned, torch in hand and followed the direction the sound had come from, listening carefully as her fear echoed still. He thought he had been unfair to her, treating her as he had. Now he prayed to Odin that he could find her before the echo faded, for he needed to apologise, to make things right.

To save her.

He turned one corner and then another, ducking low and coming out a large opening in the wall.

He scanned the room, waving his torch when the flame caught. Thyra was curled up against the wall, rocking herself back and forth, her knees tucked into her chest and arms wrapped tightly around them. The pain he had never felt before stabbed at his chest at her sight. He ran forward and rested the torch between a break in the cave wall.

"Thyra?" he asked, scooping her up into his arms. She wrapped herself around him, fighting to get closer to him.

"Sven! Trapped.... couldn't breathe....I...fear" She stumbled on the words, unable to complete a sentence. She shook in his arms and pulled her closer, cradling her head in his shoulder and shushing her as one would a frightened child.

"It's going to be all right. You are not alone," he whispered.

Eventually, she calmed and pulled herself away. When he could finally look at her face, Sven's heart sank to see her tear-stained cheeks. Sven cupped her face with his large calloused hands and stoked the tears away with his thumbs. His fingers stroked the side of her neck softly.

"Sven...Thank you....I"

"You do not need to explain. I heard your cry. I couldn't leave, despite our earlier disagreement," he said softly. He gave her the same sympathetic smile he had worn when Sören had yelled at her.

"I'm sorry you had to see me like that. I'm a sword maiden. I'm not supposed to feel fear. I wouldn't have been in these caves if it were not for you," she said, feigning anger to hide her embarrassment and grate-fulness for Sven's rescue.

"Without fear, how is one to know how to be brave?" Sven said simply.

Thyra didn't respond. This was a new thought to her, one she had not considered before.

"I apologise for my outburst earlier. However, I feel there is some-thing I should tell you. The King has offered a reward for the return of his treasure," Sven began sitting down on a rock opposite Thyra while she regained herself. He rubbed the back of his neck, struggling with a battle of his own.

Thyra's eyes widened. "Then why—"

"My father was an advisor to the King. Suddenly he fell ill, he could no longer speak, his face was no longer the one I grew up with, and he could no longer feed himself. Whatever this mystery illness that took hold of my father has crippled him," Sven said, his voice catching as he spoke of his heartbreak.

"Oh, Sven..." She reached a hand to him, taking his fingers in her own.

Sven cleared his throat and kept his eyes on the cave floor, needing to finish the story.

"My mother and older brother look after our family farm to support the family, and Revna and I took over my father's role to help as best we can. The reward is generous enough, even split six ways. It would mean my mother and brother wouldn't have to work so hard, and Revna and I could finally build our own boat and no longer be tethered to the King's vessel. Revna fears if I grow close to you, I will want to split our share. It bodes no question. If we find the treasure, it is because of your aid, so of course, I would share it with you. I explained this to Revna, but she thinks I am a fool," Sven confessed.

Thyra realised all too quickly that she had judged Revna and Sven wrong. They had a lot of troubles and were not merely greedy for gold. But nevertheless, she felt foolish herself still for how she had acted and felt a sudden warmth and admiration rush over her regarding Sven. The more she got to know him, the more she realised he was not just beautiful on the outside, but on the inside too. Sure, he had not always acted as he should, but who did? He had apologised. Could she not forgive him, especially knowing the full story?

"Revna is right. You are foolish. I have no need for coins. Besides, shouldn't we find the treasure before discussing splitting the reward?" Thyra said with a grin.

Suddenly, her face fell, as she remembered the reason she came back. The rain.

"What's wrong?" Sven asked on seeing her sudden change in demeanour.

Thyra never got a chance to answer. In the distance, she heard the rush of water filling the passageways. She was already too late.

CHAPTER 9

SVEN GRABBED the torch from the wall and took Thyra's hand. He dragged her behind him and headed up through the passage, acting as Thyra's eyes and telling her about holes in the floor and dips in the ceiling. With Sven as her guide, Thyra no longer felt her fear of the enclosed spaces and was able to follow behind with surprising ease. Sven had marked his way, and as he knew caves. It was clear she was in good hands.

As they travelled, he figured the group may head to a central passage where all the paths connected in search of each other before time ran out. They twisted and turned through passages, changing their path several times as some paths were already engulfed in water.

"He's here," yelled Ulf as he spotted Sven entering the central cavern. Sven's instincts had been right, and he breathed a sigh of relief to see everyone back together.

"I thought you left already," Revna said, more surprised than anything when she spotted Thyra behind Sven.

"I came back as soon as the storm hit. We need to leave; these caves will flood," she said.

"Several passages are already underwater. How do we get out?" Toke asked.

"This way, I marked a path but be quick," Sven said, turning back the way he'd come.

They all turned to follow Sven when Ulf stopped and bent to the floor, grabbing at something the others had missed.

"Wait! Look, it's a gold coin. It must be from the Danegeld," he yelled, raising the coin high enough for all to see.

The group stopped to look. Just then, water gushed through cracks in the ceiling. It roared as it fell, smashing against rocks and making it hard to hear each other.

"Move! Now!" Sven yelled as he took off down the passage, followed closely by the others.

They travelled down the path Sven marked but stopped suddenly as the passage they needed to take to escape was flooded. The passage was difficult enough with a low ceiling and jiggered walls. They could swim through, but it was too risky with no light. So Sven searched for another passage hoping it would double around and lead to another path to escape.

Ulf yelled out in pain as a loose rock fell from the cave's roof, smashing down on his shoulder. He grabbed his collarbone and staggered on as more water rushed through the hole in the ceiling, raising the water level to knee-deep.

The group rushed forward but found there was nowhere to go. The path they had taken led to a dead end.

"We are trapped!" Revna yelled,

"We have to go back. We will have to swim through the flooded passage; it's the only way out," Thyra yelled.

"Are you crazy? We will be swimming blind," Toke argued.

"Do you have a better idea? Please share it before we all drown," Revna barked.

"We have no choice. Come on," Sven said, turning back pushing through water that was now waist-deep.

Sven's grip on Thyra's hand tightened as they returned to the passage that dipped down, leading to their escape. He turned to her and cupped her face in his hands.

"Do you remember the twists in the passage?" he yelled above the echoing roars of rushing water in the cave. Thyra nodded.

"Take a deep breath, and don't turn back. I will be right behind you.

Go!" he said, holding the torch high so the others could easily find his location.

Thyra took a deep breath and slipped into the water, disappearing from view. Sven passed the torch to Ulf and followed closely behind Thyra. He opened his eyes underwater, but all it did was cause him pain. The cave was too dark, and the water was murky and full of debris and mud. He felt the walls relying on muscle memory for his way out. Suddenly he realised he could go no further and began to panic, he couldn't go back and was slowly running out of air. Losing hope, he felt a hand on his shoulder pulling him up. Thyra directed him to the hole in the passage leading to a higher level taking them out of the flooded passageways.

A small amount of light from the entrance called to them. It wasn't far now. Sven pulled himself from the water closely, followed by Ulf, Leif and Revna. During their swim, Leif had knocked his head, and blood spilt from his temple, staining his beard.

"Where is Toke?" Leif's voice boomed,

"He was right behind me," Revna answered, but the water lay still. There was no sign of Toke.

"I'm going back," Revna yelled,

"You can't. It is too dangerous," Leif yelled, but Revna didn't listen. Instead, she dove back into the water, quickly vanishing from sight. Everyone sat with bated breath for Revna and Toke to return. As the moments passed and the water level from the passage began to rise and chase them towards the mouth of the cave, Ulf and Leif were forced to hold Sven back as he panicked for his sister.

"She's the strongest woman I know," Ulf groaned, still gripping his injured shoulder,

"Strength means nothing if she can't breathe," Sven argued.

Revna burst out of the water in that instant, Toke bursting out behind her, shocking the group into momentary silence. Sven and Leif lunched forward, pulling Toke out of the water and leaving Revna to help herself.

"He's not breathing," Leif yelled as Revna barged past Leif pushing him aside. She grabbed Toke's face, opened his mouth, and began to breathe life into him. She pressed down on his chest several times before breathing into him again.

"Don't you dare die on me, you pig-headed fool, not after I risked my life to save you," she yelled, slamming a fist down on his chest.

Toke lurched forward, coughing muddy water and gasping for air.

"What happened?" he gasped, looking around at the sea of faces eyeing him with concern.

"Part of the passage collapsed. His foot was trapped. Now can we please leave?" Revna yelled, picking Toke up and slinging his arm over her shoulders as they all ran to the exit.

Finally, outside, they all tumbled to the ground headlong, sliding on the drenched floor as the rain continued pouring down around them. At least now they could rest easy, knowing they didn't have to worry any longer about drowning.

Allowing themselves a moment to think, they all lay still before finally scrambling to their feet. Ulf pulled the coin from his pocket, amazed that he still had it after swimming through the passage.

"We may have almost died, but we found a clue. The Danegeld is here," Ulf said, tossing the coin to Leif, who easily caught it. He played with it in between his fingers, studying the coin.

"The caves are far too wet to risk storing anything inside. He may have stored them there for a while, but chances are he moved them to the Point when he realised the caves flood. That's more likely why his man sent you there," Thyra said, and the group agreed.

"Has anyone thought to ask Halfden why he left the coin?" Thyra asked, kicking herself for not thinking of it sooner.

"Halfden left the funds for the English army. He has allies on these shores and was planning on sending word when the time came to fund the army. He was planning a war on Denmark if his plan to be rid of the King failed." Leif explained, making things all the more clear to Thyra. "It was a backup plan at best, and thankfully a plan that so far appeared to have failed," Leif continued as he tucked the coin into his pouch.

"So why can't we ask him where he left it? I'm sure if he refuses to talk, there are ways to make him," Thyra said.

"When Dittmer and Erik Jurgenson brought the Jarl to Denmark, the King had him executed for his crimes. The King now wants the money returned before someone finds it. He especially doesn't want anyone to pay off the English army. War is still a very likely possibility. Halfden had allies, some we know off, some we do not," Leif explained.

The group look around at each other. Everyone's face was one of defeat. The idea of a war on strange shores or at home with the English army, especially one funded with Danish coin, was not a pleasant thought.

"Leif!" yelled Arne, interrupting the group's sombre mood as he ran towards them with men from the town.

"Late as always," teased Toke, who hadn't taken his eyes off Revna since she saved his life. Thyra was surprised he hadn't thanked her but thought it none of her business to comment.

"You are lucky to make it out at all. The cave floods have taken many a life," one of the townsmen said as they approached.

"Come to town. We will clean you up and offer you food and a warm bed for the night," another townsman said. With little word or argument, the group groaned their agreement and headed back up the trail away from the caves.

Sven grabbed Thyra's arm and stopped her, allowing the group to walk ahead. She looked up at him questioningly and saw something In his eyes that made her heart skip a beat.

"I don't know what happened in that cave to make you so afraid, and I do not need to know if you do not wish to tell me. What I do know is it took a lot of courage to risk your life for total strangers," Sven said, pulling her closer to him.

Thyra said nothing but felt her cheeks flush red, and her body grew warm at the closeness between them despite the pair being soaked through. Sven cupped his hand around her neck and pulled her to him without a second word, bringing his soft full lips down on hers. Thyra welcomed the kiss grabbing at his clothes and pulling him closer. She opened her mouth to his allowing his tongue to explore her as she explored him.

"Shall we leave the catch up to the others later?" Sven asked, pulling away but staying close enough he could steal another kiss if he chose.

"Well, the townsfolk can lead them to the town. I am the group's guide, and I suppose I'm still sticking to orders if I guide you to a nearby cave that is dry and somewhat comfortable," she said with a wink.

She grabbed his hand and sped off up the hill, past a thicket of trees to a cave atop the mountain shielded from the rain buried deep in the mountain.

Once inside and out of the rain, Thyra led Sven through a section of wide-open passages that led to a small opening that at one point had been used to hide supplies. Blankets and other knickknacks filled the space. Unlit torches hung from several places around the area, and it took Thyra no time at all to light them. Any other time she visited this cave, she made sure to have a torch to guide her way, but with Sven by her side, she found she no longer feared the darkness.

"Let's get you out of these wet clothes," Thyra teased, reaching out and yanking Sven's shirt over his head.

"You first," Sven grinned back.

They made an easy, quick play at removing each other's clothes and the torches slowly heated up the enclosed space.

Being cold and wet meant that Thyra's nipples stood high and proud on her round pert breasts. They ached, not just from the cold but from Sven's touch.

"You are truly bewitching," Sven breathed with a wink as he admired Thyra's strong lean frame in front of him.

"You are not too bad yourself," she whispered as she ran her hands over his muscular chest, tracing a scar on his collarbone with soft, gentle kisses.

Sven sucked in a breath as Thya's tongue teased his nipples, and her hand traced the line through his abs, down past his belly button and her fingers wrapped around his swollen cock. Then, she began to stroke him painfully slowly, her hand warming him as his lips trailed kisses up his neck before taking his earlobe between her teeth.

Thyra was impressed by the length and girth of Sven and found her legs trembling at the thought of him buried deep inside her. Sven's hands ran up Thyra's muscular thighs. One stayed cupped firmly around her backside while his other hand ran up to tease her breast. She allowed her head to fall back as Sven grazed his teeth down her neck and her collarbone before taking her breast in his mouth. Thyra welcomed his warmth as the two sank to the floor made comfortable by the left-behind blankets.

Sven rolled Thyra onto her back and kissed every part of her from the top of her head to the tips of her toes. Slowly, he worked his kisses back up her legs, pushing her legs wide as he kissed her inner thighs. Finally, he looked up, keeping his eyes locked with hers as he licked his lips and gave her a mischievous grin, and he let his tongue explore her.

Thyra brought her hands to her breast, tweaking and teasing her nipples as Sven licked and sucked at the throbbing between her thighs. Thyra moaned in pleasure as she felt waves of pleasure building within her. Her moans grew louder as she drew closer to climax. Her release calling her.

Just as she was about to reach her climax, Sven pulled back and crawled up her, kissing her passionately before whispering in her ear.

"I want to feel you around me when you get your release."

His voice sent a tremble of pleasure through her.

Gently Sven pushed himself inside her, rolling his hips gently as Thyra's hands explored his muscled back. Sven stretched her in a way she had never felt before, and she groaned in pleasure, wanting and needing more.

"I want all of you, Sven," Thyra said between moans of pleasure.

"More?"

He growled the word in her ear, and she cried out, "Yes!"

Sven thrust harder and faster as Thyra's fingers clawed at his back. Sven moaned in pleasure at the moments of pain. Their moans and crying each other's names filled the cave, echoing around the small space until the two of them found their release.

EPILOGUE

BACK AT THE VILLAGE, the group settled in by the roaring fire of the inn while Revna and Thyra slept peacefully upstairs in their rooms. Leif, Sven, Ulf, Arne and Toke sat finishing their mead hunched over the table, speaking in hushed tones, not wanting anyone else to hear.

"I still don't like the fact you neglected to tell us about the potential of war. I appreciate having the full story before I accept a mission," Toke groaned.

"The mission would be the same either way. Find the coin and return it to the King," Leif said. He had been saying the same thing all evening and offering nothing else in response.

"How do we know you are not keeping other secrets from us, Leif? How do you expect us to trust you when you keep things from us?" Ulf asked as he swigged the last of his drink.

"How long have we been friends? Have you ever before had reason not to trust me?" Leif asked with a raise of an eyebrow.

"That doesn't mean we like it, Leif. You are playing your cards too close to your chest," Sven retorted.

"Now that we know about the potential of an English army, I think we should be looking for traitors in our midst. Who was the Jarl working with?" Arne asked.

"This is why I chose not to tell you. Our mission is not to find traitors but to find the Danegeld. I didn't want you to become distracted," Leif said.

Arne gave him a look. "Well, now we know, and we are here and have an opportunity to stop a war, we can't neglect that responsibility."

"We are Vikings. We do not run from a fight," Leif said gruffly.

"Running from a fight and stopping a war against our home are two very different things, my friend," Sven argued.

The discussion over what to do next went on until the early hours of the morning, well past sunset. Eventually, a decision was made. Arne and Ulf would return to the settlement and find out what they could about Halfden and his allies while Sven, Revna, Thyra, Toke and Leif continued to the Point at dawn.

THE END

REVNA

CHARMED BY A BROTHER IN ARMS

PROLOGUE

IT IS no easy thing to be rescued by the woman you've loved your entire life. Especially when the only time you've ever been in her arms was when she dragged your worthless hide out of the water, then you'd woken only to find out just one more time how much of a failure you'd been. Being a Viking, Toke had never once worried about his Mortality. He knew Valhalla awaited. He lived for battle, the adrenaline rush, and he never feared the end of anyone's blade. Toke didn't fear death. But he feared dying without settling things between himself and Revna first. But, of course, that would be even more complicated, now that she had been the one to save him.

He respected her for the warrior she was. She was just as fearsome and deadly as any Viking he had fought beside. But, at the end of the day, she was still a woman. He hated himself for thinking like that, but how else could he feel? He knew his comrades would not let him live down the fact that she had saved his worthless backside. He could hear the jokes and snippy remarks already.

The thought kept him up all night. While his friends slept, he wandered outside for some air. He kicked at the loose dirt, battling with his internal monologue. How could he ever reveal how he felt about her now? She would probably laugh in his face. How could she respect him after she was the one to save him? What does she think of him now?

The more he thought about it, the more he felt anxiety grow inside his chest, like a force crushing his lungs, not allowing him to breathe. He let out a small groan, not too loudly, out of fear of bringing unwanted attention. He paced back and forth, finally looking up to see Sven staring right at him.

"What are you doing out here?" Sven asked.

"None of your business," Toke snapped back, kicking the earth with the tip of his boot. "I couldn't sleep," he answered a little softer.

"I slept very well, but these beds are so damn small I needed to stretch my legs," Sven offered.

"I didn't ask," Toke replied, keeping his eyes cast to the ground.

"Something wrong? You are not still moping about Revna saving your ass, are you? I did offer, but she insisted it be her," Sven smiled, taking a seat on the stone step beside the door.

Toke looked up, his pained eyes finally meeting Sven. Sven's face fell, seeing how troubled his friend indeed was.

"What pains you?" he asked.

"She will never look at me, now. Things were bad before, but now? I mean, she is a strong, capable woman. Who would want to be with such a failure like me?" Toke said roughly, turning away, not wanting his friend to see the pain in his eyes.

"Is this truly about Revna? Toke, for as long as I can remember, *you* have been the one to tease and torment her. It's as if you go out of your way to piss her off. That's why she has issues with you. No other reason. If perhaps you were...I don't know....*kinder* to her. Maybe she would look your way," Sven offered.

Sven stood and walked over to his friend, who let out a gruff chuckle, not believing his friend's words.

"Or perhaps this isn't even about Revna. She doesn't see you as a failure; she sees you as a thorn in her side. Maybe you're struggling with her saving you because you worry what your father will think...." Sven ventured.

His words were cut short when Toke spun to face him, his pained face now full of anger.

"My father? Why mention him?" Toke growled.

"Leif will likely report the incident to the kind; word will get out.

That's all I meant. But, brother, it is no secret how you vie for your father's approval…."

Toke launched a punch in Sven's direction, but Sven had cat-like reflexes and jumped back in time for the strike to miss his jaw.

"Maybe you should mind your own business!" Toke snapped, storming off towards the woods.

"Where are you going?" Sven yelled after him.

"I need some air."

Sven laughed heartedly, "You are already outside."

Toke turned and waved his hands erratically, gesturing at the surrounding buildings.

"I'm in the middle of a town! How am I supposed to breathe in a crowded space like this?" Toke snapped.

His argument was weak. He just wanted to be alone with his thoughts, and Sven's words had given him plenty to think about. Now, thanks to him, he wasn't just worried about Revna, but also his father. Was this more about him than her? He punched a tree as he walked past, bark falling to the ground and his knuckle turning red. The more his mind raced, the more he felt like he couldn't breathe.

CHAPTER 1

REVNA COULDN'T GET that single coin out of her mind. It made no sense that only one coin would be there. What if the rest of the treasure was still there, but they simply missed it? They were Vikings. They shouldn't have let a little water scare them off. The fact they had left because of the flood was grating on her. It made her skin itch in frustration. If not for Toke almost drowning, she knew she could have convinced the others to stay. She tossed and turned, unable to sleep thinking about it. Eventually, she gave up trying to sleep and waited for the others to drift off.

Quietly, she crept down the stairs, passing all the other sleeping residents staying at the inn and hurried out to the barns. She had to be quick; she needed to get back before the others woke, lest they accuse her of going after the reward alone.

Entering the barn, she stroked her horse's mussel to keep her calm and quiet. Her horse was a beauty, gifted to her for their trip from the Jurgenson brothers. A tall, mighty black beast with thick white hair that covered her hooves and a luscious, thick white mane. She wished she could take the horse back to Denmark with her when their mission ended.

She saddled the horse and gathered her supplies. A sturdy rope, a lantern, and some food. She holstered her sword and tucked her blades in her boots. A proper search is needed, trying to convince herself that she was doing the right thing.

The group had plans to continue their journey come dawn. The Point awaited them. She had to move quickly; tonight was her only chance to search the caverns. She let her imagination wander as she packed her things into the saddlebags. What would it be like to find the treasure? How much would she find? Before the Jarl was executed for his crimes against the King, they found out about his habit of stealing from the Danegeld. His men knew of his doings, but none knew precisely how much had been taken and hidden away. They knew it was enough to potentially fund an army. Would she find a cavern so full it was bursting with gold? Had coin been the only thing she stole?

She imagined stumbling across a cavern the size of the entire inn, filled with trunks of gold and jewels. She imagined art and weapons. Anything and everything the Jarl would deem valuable. Her skin prickled with goosebumps. The world would know her name after such a find. Then another thought occurred to her. Would she have to split the reward? If she ventured out alone and discovered it independently, wouldn't the reward be hers and hers alone?

The world would be hers if the reward went to her alone. She could give an amount to her family and then get her own boat and sail the world. She could start a community of her own, made of strong women to raid with. No one would be able to stop them. Her heart began to race, and the hairs on the back of her neck stood on end. Excitement rushed through her. She felt drunk on the thought alone. It was intoxicating, the idea of freedom.

"Come on, girl, let's go," she whispered to her horse.

Grabbing the reigns, she prepared to mount, but the night had other plans. She was seized by the shoulders and pulled away. She spun around, ready to fight, her face full of thunder when she came face to face with Toke. His face was red with fury, and his brow furrowed so deep his eyebrows almost touched his nose and caused his forehead to crease.

"And where do you think you are going?" he snapped.

CHAPTER 2

TOKE MAY SEEM stupid but he was no fool. He knew precisely why Revna was out now, and he knew exactly what she planned to do. He had to admit, he was impressed with her planning and execution, but he was angry that he hadn't thought of it first.

Finding the Jarl's hoard would raise his status immensely. Revna would be forced to take note of him then. But, Revna aside, it would make his father – an advisor to the King – stand up and take notice. Toke had a shaky relationship with his father. No matter what he did, he was a failure in his father's eyes.

"A useless, pathetic excuse for a Viking," was one of the last things his father said to him before he took the mission with Lief and the others. He imagined the look on his father's face when he walked in to accept his reward and told of the glory of returning the King's coin to him.

"What are you doing here?" Revna snapped, pushing his hands off her.

"Never mind me. Are you going after the treasure alone? Why? To claim the reward as your own?" Toke whispered angrily.

Neither of them wanted to be caught.

"I'm sorry, do I need your permission to do my job? It makes no difference if I go alone or go with a group. We leave for the Point at dawn. I'm continuing what we started before I had to save your hide. I might not find anything, but I have to try. As long as I'm back by morning, what does it matter?" she spat back, jabbing a finger into his shoulder hard before turning back to her horse.

Toke smirked at her. It was a poor argument, shaky at best. He did agree she made sense, but he would never tell her that.

"You are not going to that cave, not without me anyway. So, I'm going with," he said, pushing past her to saddle up his horse.

"Like Helheim, you are. I'm not a child who needs watching, and I'm not one of those prissy ladies of the court who needs a man constantly at her side. I could have you hogtied and left here till morning if I wanted." She snapped.

Toke was glad he had his back to her. While he wasn't one to enjoy it when a woman took the lead, he felt himself stare at the thought of her binding him and doing whatever she pleased.

"Calm yourself, woman. I do not doubt your abilities. Nor do I wish to protect you. The caverns are dangerous, and Sven would have my head on a spike if he found out I let you go alone, if something were to happen to you." Toke said, mounting his horse and watching, waiting for her to react.

She huffed out a groan of annoyance before reluctantly admitting defeat.

"Fine," she growled through clenched teeth.

She mounted her horse and headed out at speed, leaving Toke to catch up.

CHAPTER 3

Revna steamed as she galloped off out of town and into the forest. She neither needed nor wanted his help. She especially didn't need help from a stupid Viking who can't even watch where he is going. Her point was proven when she heard him yelp as a low hanging branch smacked him in the face while he was racing after her. If she weren't so angry at him, she would have laughed. But instead, she rolled her eyes and kicked her horse a little more swiftly, increasing its speed and the distance between them.

As the caves came into view down the hill, her mind flashed back to yesterday. She felt the panic she had when she realised when he wasn't coming up from the hole—the thought of his drowning in that dark pit, alone and scared. Toke and Revna didn't see eye to eye on most things. He disagreed with everything she ever said and belittled her at every opportunity. She thought he was an immature, pompous ass. But once, long ago, there had been something there. Even if she didn't like the man he has turned into, a deep-seated part of her still burns for him. She still craves his touch and longs to see him smile at her. She hated that part of herself. It was soppy and too much like the behaviour of the English ladies of the court. Not the actions or behaviours of an intense sword maiden who had many a victory in battle.

She dismounted and tied her steed to a tree, staring into the abyss of the cave. Panic once again set in. She was lucky to save him last time. What if she couldn't protect him again? She glanced back and saw how close he was to catching up. She didn't want to risk losing him in the maze of caverns. She couldn't live with the guilt if he didn't make it out alive.

She remembered the day before, after she had dragged him from the pool. She remembered breathing into him and pounding on his chest. The emptiness of thinking his eyes had closed forever. She never wanted to relive that feeling.

Toke dismounted and left his stead with hers, taking long strides to join her at the mouth of the cave. He took a step to go inside, and she reached out, placing a hand on his chest and froze at the muscle she felt under her fingertips. She hoped her face didn't reveal her surprise at the fire that ran through her veins.

"Perhaps you should go back and wake the others," she ventured, unsure of what argument she could present to stop him from joining her.

"Why not say that before we left? We are here now. Come on, let's get it over with so we can head back to the inn's warmth," he said, trying to push past her, but she held her grip and stance.

"I will say this only once, and also because there is no one else around to hear, so no one will believe you. You were right. I shouldn't have come here alone. Go back and get the others; there are too many caverns for the two of us to search." She tried again.

Toke took a step back, watching her intently. He folded his arms across his chest, and his face mirrored the expression of anger he shot at her when he found her in the barn.

"I thought better of you, Revna," he tsked, shaking his head slowly with disapproval.

"Excuse me?"

"Are you so greedy to risk life and limb in these caves alone? You would risk being trapped in the dark, drowning in a sunken cavern or whatever fresh hell awaits your fate. Just to find the treasure alone? You are no better than the Jarl," he snarled.

Toke had said some pretty shocking and awful things to her in the past. Yet nothing had cut as deep as that statement. She was hurt. Deeply. She felt her anger rile inside her like a caged bear.

"You would risk just as much, if not more, if it meant your father would give you a second look," she sneered.

No sooner did the words leave her lips did the voice in the back of her mind scold her for going too far. It was a low blow, even for her. Toke's relationship with his father was well known, and it was known by those closest to him how much of a sore subject it was. She regretted it instantly. She opened her mouth to apologise, but before she could even blink, Toke snatched the lantern from her hand and stormed off into the caves.

She watched the light of the lantern fade from view, still stunned by her petty stupidness. She needed to apologise. Differences aside, Toke wasn't all bad. And even so, he didn't deserve the poison she shot at him with the snap of her tongue.

CHAPTER 4

REVNA AND TOKE had grown up together. And she thought about those times together all those years ago as she chanced after him. Trying to find the words to apologise wasn't easy, especially when the wound was deep. Revna remembered standing on her family's farm and watching as Toke did everything he could to make his father proud, but nothing seemed to be enough. Their neighbouring farmland lent itself to Toke's consistent wanderings, desperate to think of a way to win his father's approval. She thought back to the time when they fought playfully with their swords, preparing for battles not even dreamt about. She thought back to the time when she told herself she would be the greatest sword maiden and put Toke's father in his place. Toke's father had been pretty rough on him; their shaky history was well known throughout the kingdom. With his father being such a close advisor to the King, it was hard to hide the distance and disapproval between father and son.

Toke and Revna used to be close. They used to share apples from harvest and horse rides on watch duty. But as they grew, his father's lashings and vicious tongue tore Toke down and he began to take the frustrations he had towards his father out on Revna. He grew from a companion into her bully, even if she could hold her own. And she still wished she could have helped him somehow.

Before they were teamed up for this mission, it had been a while since the pair had seen each other. She wondered if his relationship with his father had gotten worse, wondered what else had happened in his life. The guilt and absence began to eat away at her. *Did it eat away at him too?* She shook the thought off. He deserved to be told off for accusing her of such things, but she could have handled it in a better way. She remembered how his words had hurt her as a child, and she didn't want history to repeat itself.

She hurried after him using muscle memory alone. With Toke so far ahead with the only lantern, it was hard to see the dim light. She called for him several times when she finally caught up, but he ignored her. Even though her temper flared, Revna found that her heart ached at how he dismissed her. Finally, she grabbed his shoulder, trying to pull him to a stop.

"Toke, I'm sorry, I was out of line. You touched a nerve, and I reacted badly. Please, let me apologise," she pleaded.

Toke grunted and shrugged his shoulder out of her grip, still not wanting to look at her. *Why does it bother me so much?* She didn't want them to fall out over this. He was a pompous ass at times, but he was still her friend. One of her oldest friends.

"Toke, stop being so stubborn and look at me. I'm telling you how sorry I am. I didn't mean it." She insisted, grabbing him harder and spinning him around.

Toke's foot slipped on the moss-covered floor, and he stumbled towards her. It took a few steps to regain his footing, but when he had, his eyes widened, realising how close they were.

He was in her arms, their noses practically touching. His heart pounded in his chest as they locked eyes. He noticed soft brown freckles he had not seen before, as the light of the lantern shone in her eyes. A breeze travelled throughout the cave, bringing her scent with it. It filled his nostrils. She was intoxicating. He noticed how she did not attempt to push him away. She liked him being so close. Her chest heaved, and he felt her breasts stroke his chest with each full breath she took.

Neither of them knew how, or who made the first move, but suddenly, their lips locked. At first, it started tender and nervous, each figuring out how the other felt. Then tongues entangled in a tango of unspoken words and pent-up feelings. Finally, they kissed long and hard, neither wanting it to end.

Slowly they pulled apart, staring at each other, waiting for who might speak the first words. They panted for breath, still riding the high of their kiss. Then, stunned, they stood basking in the light from the lantern, amazed by such a turn of events.

"You were right," Toke breathed, his eyes going wide.

"No, I wasn't, that's the point..." she began to protest.

Toke patted her shoulder and the corner of his mouth creased into a grin. Revna didn't know what shocked her more, the kiss or his attempt at a smile. Smiling was something Toke never did. He was consistently severe and all business in his interactions with others, even among the closest of friends in the group.

"Not about that. You were an ass. That we can agree. But, look," he said, pointing at the high ledge just over her shoulder.

Walking past her, he raised the lantern to get a better look; light bounced off the single gold coin.

"We were further in the caverns when we found the first one. How is this here?" Revna asked.

"It doesn't matter. The point is Revna. You were right to come back." He answered.

CHAPTER 5

"I CAN'T REACH. You'll have to climb up and see what's there," Toke said as he placed the lantern down on a rock. "I'll give you a boost," he said, taking her by the waist and raising her high with little effort.

Revna's skin broke out into goosebumps at his touch and display of strength. Her head still spun from the kiss. *What did it mean? Did he enjoy it as much as her?* She still couldn't remember who moved in first.

Reaching, she grabbed the ledge and pulled herself up. Turning back, she grabbed the lantern from Toke's outstretched hand and lit up the area. There was a small opening, and yet again, only one coin was in sight. She sank to her belly and shimmied further inside to get a better view, but the opening was narrow, and she could see much further, reaching blind in the dark. She felt around, but her hand met nothing but a wall.

"What do you see?" Toke asked.

"Nothing, just the one coin. There is some debris but nothing else," she answered.

She could have come down, but she wasn't thinking clearly. Her mind was no longer on the Jarl's hoard or the reward. All she could think about was that kiss. The kiss she could still feel on her lips and taste on her tongue. Did she hold feelings for Toke all this time and had just ignored them? Did he carry a torch for her?

"Revna!" Toke yelled, bringing her back into the room.

"What? Sorry, I can't hear you," she sputtered.

"I said, could someone have placed it there to throw us off the trail? Do you think someone else knows about our mission?" he answered. She didn't miss the exasperated tone of his voice.

"I don't know, but there is a ton of debris here." She answered, crawling backwards to make her way down.

"That means nothing," Toke dismissed.

She crawled backwards and let her legs dangle until her feet hit a ledge so she could climb down. Toke once again grabbed her waist and helped her down. Her skin shivered at his touch. Standing face to face, the tension was thick. The only sound in the caves was their slow breathing and the odd drip of water still left from the floods.

"Revna….that kiss…." Toke began softly.

Revna panicked, not wanting to talk about it. She couldn't think straight and didn't want to say anything that might make things awkward. They could speak once she had time to process, but not here. Not in the dark cave.

"A rat probably brought it up there. Maybe that's why we only ever find the one discarded coin. Rats are probably making off with the hoard," she offered in haste.

She kicked herself mentally; it was a stupid answer, but the more he touched her, the more she found her mind reeling. She couldn't think straight and shot out any lame idea that came into her head. Rubbing the debris and stone off her clothes, she finally glanced up and saw Toke's unamused face.

"What?" she asked.

"Rats? Is that the best you can come up with?"

"Do you have a better explanation?" she asked.

"Are we really not going to talk about what just happened? I thought you women like to talk about such things," he said, trying, and failing, to hide his growing amusement.

He knew he had rattled her; she was not herself. She felt it too and pushed forward with her argument.

"Humour me. Look for droppings, we can find out where the rats are coming from, and they could lead us to the rest of the gold," she said, trying to sound as confident as she could.

Toke wasn't fooled, but obliged. He rolled his eyes and took the lantern from her, scouring the floor for anything resembling rat droppings.

"This is stupid. First, it's dark as night here. How am I supposed to see something as small as a rat dropping? Secondly, rats do not run off with gold," he argued in frustration, finally giving up on his search.

"Please, if you have a better plan, tell me," she said.

"Why aren't you looking too? Why am I the one who has to look for rat shit?" he groaned.

Revna said nothing for a moment until she realised he was genuinely waiting for an answer. "You have the lantern."

Toke rolled his eyes. He was getting annoyed. His body ached with pent-up tension brought on by their kiss. He wanted to talk about it so he knew how she felt, and so they could do it again.

"I thought you were smarter than this Revna."

"What?"

"You are a grown woman. A Viking woman. One of the best sword maidens I know. Yet we kiss, and suddenly you turn into a child. Offering stupid ideas and shaky arguments. I thought better of you. I guess I was wrong," Toke shrugged.

He knew what he was doing; trying to make her mad. To get any kind of reaction from her. With any Viking, be it a man or woman, the best place to poke the bear is through the ego. As expected, she took the bait.

"Call me stupid one more time. I dare you!" she snarled.

"I never said you were stupid. I said your idea was stupid. There is a difference. Woman!"

That's all it took. The derogatory tone and emphasis behind the simple word – woman. She was a woman and a damn good one. But if you put the focus in the right place, you can turn any word into an expression of animosity. Revna's blood boiled. She didn't like how he tried to take her power; it felt demeaning.

Her arm reeled back and flew through the air. The sound of her hand slapping against his cheek echoed through the cavern. Toke hadn't expected her to react like that and stood, stunned in place.

With the last dying echos of flesh connecting with flesh, Revna gave in to her desires and grabbed Toke's collar with both hands, yanking him close. She kissed him harshly, and much to her pleasure, he kissed back with just as much force. His hands wound up in her hair, pulling at the roots and trying to drag her closer. Their tongues massaged each other madly, savouring the taste of their desires.

Toke shoved her back, and she smacked into the cave wall, the hunger and lust in his eyes making the force a pain she was willing to endure. Their mouths met again as their hands explored each other wildly. Years of pent-up sexual tension and words needing to be spoken. Everything they were too afraid to say out loud was in that kiss.

CHAPTER 6

THE TENSION ROSE, thick and fast. Their breathing grew heavy. They both knew what was coming, and they both wanted it. Toke's hand ran up Revna's body, cupping her breasts. He revelled in the feeling of her filling his hand.

Revna could feel her nipples grow pert at his touch. She craved to feel his hands on her bare skin. She reached for his shirt and tore it open, pushing it off his large, bulging shoulders, running her hands over the wall of muscle that was his chest. He sucked in a breath as her hands ran down his chest, hiding that he trembled at her touch, with anticipation.

Toke ripped open her shirt and buried his face in her neck, nipping and kissing her collar bone, trailing his way up to her ear. His hand slipped into her shirt and pawed at her breast. He gripped her aching nipple between his finger and thumb and began to play as she moaned with pleasure.

They still wore far too much clothing. She needed to feel him against her. Flesh on flesh. She pushed him back and grinned at his momentary shock before his eyes twinkled, catching the knowing glint in her eye. She quickly ripped off the rest of her clothes, and he hurried to match her speed of undress.

Toke cursed the lantern's dim light; he could outline her tall, muscular yet feminine frame. The curves of her hips, the fulness of her breasts,. He wished he could see all of her. But he was happy for his hands to be his eyes for the time being.

She gazed at his godlike frame, the way the light highlighted the perfect v descending his hips, pointing towards the main attraction. The way it twitched at the sight of her. He was thicker than she imagined, and she ached to feel him stretch her open. Stepping forward, she took him in her hand, enjoying the groan he let out at her touch. She ran her hand along his length, savouring the feeling of him powerless beneath her fingers.

He grabbed her arms and pulled her closer, taking her breasts in hand and guiding her aching nipples into his mouth. Nipping the throbbing flesh, he licked them with his tongue. Their moans of pleasure pierced the stillness. He loved hearing her moan and wanted her to cry louder and scream his name as she clenched herself around him. The more he thought of it, the harder he became, the more her touch agonised him in the best possible way.

Toke ran a hand down her body, loving how she moved with the trail of his fingers. He slipped his hand between her thighs, grinding against her as his lips trailed kisses from her breast to her neck. He loved how the pleasure of his touch ran down her thighs. He wanted to make that feeling last as long as possible. His ego grew, knowing her body's response was because of him touching her. She was already wet, waiting for him. She needed him, wanted him.

He teased her as she teased him, stroking his fingers over her and running circles over the bud that swelled for his touch. She felt her legs begin to tremble and her grip on him tighten. Toke felt himself growing as Revna stroked him. He struggled to keep his knees from buckling as she teased his tip with her thumb.

"Revna...I..." he began, but Revna cut him off with a passionate kiss, letting her tongue invade his mouth.

Toke slipped a finger inside, relishing as her sweetness ran over his hand, and she moaned against his mouth. It wasn't enough; he needed to feel her on top of him. He needed to feel himself inside her. Gently taking her by the hips, he walked her backwards to a boulder and spun her around. He pushed her legs apart and stroked the firm roundness of her backside, giving her a small smack that made her jump and moan from the pleasure of the pain.

"I need to feel you, Toke..." she moaned as he took hold of himself.

His mind raced; he worried he wouldn't be able to last long as she drove him crazy already. Just a few strokes inside her, he knew he would spill himself. He aimed himself at her entrance, bracing for glory when their lust bubble was burst.

Shouting from a cavern through the passages alerted them that they were not alone. Who was it? They didn't recognise the voices and couldn't hear what was being yelled clear enough. Revna spun, lust in her eyes and pain on her face. She had been ready for him, and their time had been cut short.

"We will get back to this later," Toke winked as the pair made haste at reclothing.

Their eyes never left each other as they redressed. Of course, it was a lot more fun in reverse, but now they both knew of the beauty hidden by their garments; images that wouldn't leave their minds anytime soon.

Toke clenched his jaw, trying to hide his frustration as his hard cock strained against the fabric. Revna winced as the wool of her tunic scraped her pert aching nipples.

If only they had a little longer. How glorious it would have been.

CHAPTER 7

"IT HAS to be the others. They must have discovered we left." Revna panicked, as she finished fastening her belt.

The last thing she wanted was their help. She had been reluctant to accept Toke's help, and only did because he insisted she not go alone. But, thinking it through, she quickly realised that she had a lot more in common with Toke than she first thought. He did everything he could to win the approval of his father, and she always did whatever she could to prove herself to the world. She was a Viking woman, a sword maiden, and a strong warrior. But she was still a woman in the eyes of the world. And women always had to try harder to prove themselves.

The money, the reward, the boat. All her reasons for coming back to the cave came flooding back. Her mind was back on her mission. Absentmindedly, she mumbled away to herself.

"Revna, we are a team. We all have the same mission, sent by the King. We have to do what is right for the group." Toke reminded her gently. She hadn't expected him to hear her ramblings.

"Are you against me, Toke? Still believing I'm greedy and self-centred?" she snapped as she fastened her boot, tucking her blade back inside.

Toke sighed and shook his head; he grew tired of the same old argument. He was sure he had convinced her that he was on her side this time.

"Of course not," he breathed, following her deeper into the caverns.

They followed the echoing of the voices, searching passage after passage. The caverns were a maze of twists and turns. Thankfully, they remembered their path from the day prior, or they would have gotten lost. They searched the caverns they entered the day before. While they found new caverns, they found nothing else.

"Maybe I was wrong to try and search again. There is nothing here," Reina said in frustration.

"We found another coin. There must be something here, don't doubt yourself. Your instincts were right," Toke tried to reassure her.

"One coin. Nothing else...." She stopped, as they entered a cavern they had not seen before. The cavern was small and cramped and would be easily hidden by fallen rocks that lay stacked blocking the entrance.

There was evidence that someone had been there before. Several rotting corpses, the smell thick and choking. A handful of coins but nothing more. The money had been there. They were sure of it now. Someone had moved it, but who? And where was it now?

Revna stopped in her tracks, stunned. The corpses were a mess. One was missing an arm that lay close by. Another with a mangled leg. There were two more further back. One had an axe impaled through his helm, and another slumped with a spear embedded in their chest. A nasty battle occurred here. They had been left to bleed and slowly starve. It was a horrible way to die, a cruel and empty dishonourable death.

Toke crept up behind her and wrapped his arms around her, pulling her into his embrace. He could see she was struggling with the sight before them.

"What do you see?" he asked, his breath tickling her ear.

"I...."

"Do you want me to tell you what I see?" he asked, pointing at the scene. "The Jarl's men. They had been tasked to protect the hoard. When no one came to claim it, they argued over the gold. It ended badly in death," he began. "Is this an honourable way to act? Is it an honourable death? Are these men feasting in Valhalla?" he asked, allowing her to come to her own conclusions.

Toke didn't want to force his opinions. He liked that Revna had her own mind. She sighed against him, trying not to choke on the smell of decaying, rotting flesh.

"You are right. We need to find the others. We share a goal for the King and Denmark," she yielded. "I can hear the others approaching," she breathed, saddened that their time alone had once again been cut short.

She turned to face him and smiled softly. She saw a new softer side to Toke, but he was still the man she had grown to admire. He, too, was seeing her in a new light. She was strong, determined, and had a beautiful mind.

Footsteps grew louder, and boots smashed against stone and splashed in shallow puddles. The light of several lanterns danced at the entrance as they drew closer. It was time for Revna to face the music. She had to admit to herself, her brother, and the others that she had come here for selfish reasons. She had since changed her mind and was back united with their goal.

"I better apologise," she said, stepping around Toke.

A figure pushed through the entrance, unclear in the darkness of the passage. Revna assumed, from its size, that it was Leif. She opened her mouth to fight her case, but his face became apparent as the figure raised his lantern. It wasn't Leif. It was someone else entirely.

CHAPTER 8

EIGHT MEN STEPPED into the caverns. Brits? Highlanders? Kelts? It was unclear. One clear thing was that the Vikings were no longer the only ones who knew about the treasure. These men were not Vikings. They dressed in plain hunting gear, and their weapons looked weak. Revna wondered if any of them had ever held a sword in actual battle.

"Who are you?" one of the men asked, his voice booming, bouncing off the walls.

"I could ask you the same question," Toke snarled, joining Revna.

"What are you doing here? State your business!" Revna snapped.

"Our business is ours alone." One of them answered.

It was apparent they searched for the same thing. Revna noted how their eyes drifted passed her to the small selection of coins scattered on the floor.

"They know of our search. They have seen our faces." "We can't let them leave," the group argued.

Toke nudged Revna with his elbow and dropped his eye to the axe at her hip. She nodded back in agreement. They were going to have to fight their way out. Toke let his hand rest on the hilt of knives on his belt; he wished he had brought his sword with him. Placing the lantern on a high ledge allowing the light to illuminate the room a little more, he scanned his surroundings. Dips in the floor, jiggered rocks, ridges, and puddles. He noted the parts of floor covered in slippery moss. All traps and pitfalls he planned to use to his advantage.

"Kill them," one from the group said. But Revna and Toke lept into action before any of them could react.

Revna pulled her axe from her hip and a knife from her boot. In one swift motion, she threw the blade through the air, embedding it in one man's throat. He clenched at the knife with eyes wide open, gurgling as he choked on his own blood, life slipping through his fingers. She yanked the spear from the rotting corpse and flung it with another quick turn. It struck the taller man in the leg knocking him to the floor. His screams sounded even higher in the small space. Toke grabbed the sword at the man's hip and swung it, taking his head off his shoulders.

The rest of the group moved swiftly to surround Toke and Revna. They stood back-to-back fighting. The men were more skilled than Revna first assumed; she had underestimated them and cried out as a blade sliced through her arm. Toke spun; hearing her scream, he pushed her aside and ran the man through. Revna grabbed the knife and jammed it under the chin of the one who approached her from the left.

Four down, four to go, Toke thought.

The last four fought harder. They dodged attacks and swung their weapons in an onslaught of vicious, fast movements. Revna had since lost two of her blades, as they lay in the bleeding bodies of their enemies. The rest of her weapons were back at the inn. She hadn't been prepared for a battle like this, armed with only one small axe.

Several of the men's lanterns had been smashed in the struggle. The only light from the one lantern left, Toke had put up high. Lack of light made fighting the enemy that much more complicated. A few times, Revna had almost mistaken Toke for the attackers. The floor was uneven and slippery, making it challenging to manoeuvre without tripping.

Tokes back ached. Revna's shoulder was sore. They had fought so hard, and Revna was convinced dawn was approaching. But there was no way to tell how much time had passed this deep in the cavern.

Toke had a gash on his thigh and two in the shoulder. Revna's arm still bled, and she now wore a new scar across her cheek. More footsteps echoed from outside the passage entrance. The group was more significant than first thought. At least five more men entered. Toke and Revna were unsure of how many due to lack of light. Things looked grim. Outnumbered and out armed.

"Toke," Revna whispered, reaching out to touch his hand.

Toke grabbed it and held it tight. Their eyes locked as they silently said goodbye. If this were the end, they would go out fighting. They would die with honour. The Viking way. Revna felt her eyes sting with tears she didn't want to shed. They had come so far that night. Hope was sparked only to be extinguished without getting any real answers. There was so much she wanted to say, but instead, she tried to remember the lines of his face, the sparkle in his eyes, and the soft smile her offered only to her.

We will be together in Valhalla, she thought.

"Take as many down as you can. Make them regret crossing a Viking," Toke said, and Revna nodded her agreement as they launched back into battle.

One man fell, then another. Suddenly Toke heard it; he glanced back and saw Revna had heard it. Rushing water. Was it raining? Were the caverns about to flood? With a swing of a stolen sword, Toke sliced open the man's gut that he fought before running back and grabbing Revna, pulling her tightly to him.

"Do you trust me?" he yelled.

"Yes," she answered.

Toke sent the lantern flying across the room with a swing of his sword. Its light vanished as it smashed into the face of the man who ran towards them. The room was completely black. A darkness Revna had never seen before. It was unsettling, terrifying that there was nothing but emptiness. A shiver ran down her spine; *these were the conditions that the Jarl's men died in, and for what?* She thought.

CHAPTER 9

"MY EYES!" screamed the voice of Toke's latest victim. His agonising screams followed them as Toke blindly guided Revna through the passageways.

He had paid much more attention to the twists and turns of the cave than he had the day before. Running blind with an outstretched hand, he felt his way through. He was ducking under the lower passageways and instructing Revna to grip hold of his belt when they were forced to crawl through tighter ridges.

"This next passage dips below, be careful when you descend on the other side," Toke said.

As he descended, he noticed Revna no longer held fast to him. His heart pounded so hard he could hear it in his ears. He felt around but couldn't find her. His mind flashed; was this how she had felt when he didn't follow from the waters? Anxious, he crawled back inside the ridge but couldn't touch her.

"Revna!" he yelled in panic.

"I am here, I just lost my grip. I can't see you," came her voice.

He turned and smashed into her; the two shared a brief chuckle before Toke once again grabbed her hand and took off through the passages. Turning when needed and quickly coming upon the path from the day before. The water was not so deep this time, a lot easier to swing through. But if the water continued to flow soon enough, it would be just as deadly as when he almost drowned.

Toke froze, remembering that he had been trapped under the chilled waters when he reached out and found no one there. The next thing he remembered was Revna pounding on his chest.

"I'm right behind you," she assured him.

The angry yells and groans grew louder. Cries of pain as the following group tripped and smashed into walls blindly. They might not have known the caverns quite as well as Toke and Revna, but it would not be long before they found them. Toke said nothing and made no effort to move. Revna pulled the rope from her belt, quickly tying it around herself and then around Toke. Revna worried that they would not escape the group a second time if he waited much longer.

"We go in together. We come out together," she said with a nod, easing herself into the waters and waiting for Toke to follow.

Together they swam, guiding each other, resting, assured they were not alone. Finally, they climbed out the other side. Revna quickly unshackled them from each other. The cave's entrance was finally in sight. Dawn shone through, guiding them on their way out.

They ran to the entrance and saw Leif, Sven, Ulf, and Arne heading towards them. While the sun shone, it was still raining. If it continued, the caves would flood. Several horses grazed nearby, and Toke and Revna came to the same conclusion.

"There is more of them in the caves," Toke said.

"At least twenty by the looks of these tracks," Revna gasped, pointing to the many footsteps in the mud.

"We need to seal the cave," Toke yelled and dragged boulders and rocks across the cave's entrance. The ground was still soft from the rain overnight and even softer now. Without hesitation, Leif and the group obliged and began blocking the access. Revna could still hear yells coming from inside the cave.

They are not moving quick enough, Revna thought.

She looked up at the trees above the mouth of the cave. Then, an idea occurred to her—a landslide.

"Toke...." she yelled.

She ran up the hill and Toke swiftly followed.

"We need to create a landslide. Then, seal the cave properly," she urged.

"Everyone out of the way!" Toke yelled.

Together Toke and Revna loosened a boulder and jabbed at the soft earth, doing everything they could to crumble the ground beneath them. The edge of the clip crumbled, and Toke grabbed Revna to stop her from being dragged over the edge. They ran back down the hill and joined the others as they watched the heavy rain bring more of the cliff above the rim. They were closing the cave and sealing everyone inside for good.

"Now. What the hell was all that about?" Sven huffed for breath, searching the face of his sister and his friend.

CHAPTER 10

"WE ARE NOT the only ones seeking the Jarl's hoard," Toke warned.

"What do you mean?" Lief asked.

Toke and Revna told the group about their attackers and how they appeared to know where the gold had once been kept. They explained they couldn't tell who their attackers were, be it the Brits, the Celts or someone else.

"Is the treasure lost?" Arne asked.

"I believe it was once here but no longer is. So we should continue to the Point," Revna answered.

"You should have let them come. Let them meet their end by the hand of Vikings," Ulf groaned.

"The best thing to do was seal them in the cave. We may have escaped for now, but if we don't know who they are, we also don't know how many. What if they had an army just waiting to return with the gold? Imagine if they told whomever they work for that the Vikings also seek the stolen Danegeld." Toke said.

"Toke and Revna are right. You did the right thing sealing the cave. They are our enemies, not our equals," Leif began. "But I beg the question, what were you two doing down here anyway? Why leave in the middle of the night? Is there something I need to be informed of?"

Toke glanced at Revna, waiting for her to speak. She stepped forward, her head bowed and took a breath before allowing her gaze to meet the rest of the group.

"I couldn't sleep thinking about that one coin. I felt I could track down the treasure on my own. It was stupid and selfish and greedy on my part. My intentions may have started from self-satisfaction, but I assure you my loyalty is to the group, to this mission," Revna said, bowing her head again.

She half expected Lief to give her a tongue lashing or dole out some other form of punishment for betraying her commanding officer. But before Lief could speak, Toke stood by her side. He stood proud and strong and, much to the group's utter disbelief, came to Revna's defence.

"I, too, must take responsibility. I saw Revna leaving, and rather than stop her; I insisted she not go alone. It might not have been the best course of action in hindsight, but I'm glad I came with her. The outcome may not have been what we seek, but we have at least eliminated a dead end and learnt more about our enemies."

Leif raised an eyebrow while the others stood opened mouthed, shocked by the sudden turn of events. Toke and Revna were no longer at each other's throats. Sven, in particular, never thought he would see the day.

"It doesn't seem likely that multiple groups would be looking for the hoard, right? Surely the Jarl was not stupid enough to tell so many," Sven offered.

"What if it is the army of which you speak," Ulf said to Lief.

"Who else could it be?" Arne asked.

"The Brits? It would make sense, given how he sided with them before. The Celts? Unlikely, we have a shaky relationship with them as it is. Highlanders? Or someone else entirely?" Sven pondered.

The group fell silent. All felt uneasy. They knew they would need to face new enemies on these shores, but the real question was, who was the enemy? Could the Jurgenson brothers be involved? An enemy disguised as a friend? No one wanted to think of the possibilities. They all wanted to find the haul and head home, back to Denmark.

"We must make haste. Get to the Point as quickly as possible and find the Danegeld before anyone else," Leif said, nodding his orders.

Everyone grunted their agreement before mounting their horses.

Revna and Toke shared stolen glances, mindful of the ever-watching eyes of Sven and the others. So much was left unspoken and unfinished in the cave. Adrenaline and lust were still thick on their tongues, made even sweeter by the rush of battle.

"Sven, will Thyra still guide us to the Point?" Toke asked.

"She will," Sven nodded.

"We better gather supplies then. Fully prepare for the journey and any surprises it may bring," said Revna.

"Agreed. Come now, we have much to prepare," Lief stated, spurring his horse onwards.

The others swiftly followed, but as Revna went to gallop her horse, Toke reached out and stopped her.

"Let us catch up with them later. They do not need our help gathering supplies. What is it the women say? Too many cooks?" Toke winked, a slight grin creasing his lips.

If Revna knew any better, she would swear he was trying to smile, but she doubted it. He was a man who rarely smiled. A part of her wanted to see him smile. To see his eyes crease with happiness. The thought both scared and warmed her.

"It's raining," Revna answered.

"So?" Toke shrugged. "Is the mighty warrior queen Revna scared of a little rain? You are a Viking after all."

Revna realised what he was insinuating, but she wanted to hear it from him. To listen to the words pass his lips. She watched as he dismounted, taking a few strides to be standing in front of her.

"What do you have in mind?" She purred as he plucked her off her horse, placing her gently feet first in front of him.

"I want to finish what we started in that cave," he growled in her ear.

His breath on her neck and the memories of his touch sent a chill down her spine. As delicious as honey and as hot as fire. She closed her eyes and let his hands travel up the side of her body as his lips lay kisses along her neck.

"And what was that exactly?" she asked.

"Come, Revna, no need to play coy," he teased.

"Tell me, Toke. Tell me what you wanted to do to me in that cave," she breathed.

Toke stepped back and looked at her; he was happy she was willing, but he never thought her desires were as strong as his. Her eyes drooped with lust, and she clenched her bottom lip between her teeth.

"I wanted to...I wanted..." Toke found he was lost for words. He knew what he wanted, but Revna had rendered him speechless.

"Ok, then let me tell you what I wanted...." She began, slowly pulling off her clothes as she did.

Toke had never been so happy to see the light of day. He could see all of her, no longer hidden in the cave's darkness. Her large breasts that were more than a handful sat proudly high on her chest. He couldn't wait to have the muscles in her legs wrapped around his waist, the angles of her hips, and the curves of her backside. She was magnificent. Her nipples stood tall in the chill of the rain; Toke would never forget how she moaned as he toyed with her.

"I wanted to feel you grow in my hands....I wanted to taste you and hear you scream my name....." she whispered as she slowly peeled his clothes off his body. "I wanted to feel you stretch me. I wanted you to fuck me like it was your last night before joining your ancestors in Valhalla. I wanted the gods to hear you cry my name as you lost yourself inside me."

Toke had been so mesmerised by her words. So lost in the picture she was painting that he hadn't realised he now stood shirtless with his pants around his ankles. He let out a moan deep from his throat as Revna took hold of his throbbing cock in her hand.

"Revna. I never knew you....that...." He stuttered.

"What? That I like sex as much as you men do?" she purred in his ear. "So, tell me, Toke, what do you want?" she purred, stroking the length of him faster.

He could feel himself growing harder, his pleasure building at her touch. But Toke had never been good with words. He grabbed her by the shoulders and spun her around, shoving her back hard against a sizeable thick tree.

"I'm not a poet. I've never been good with words. So I let my actions speak for me," he growled before he brought his lips crashing down on hers.

Revna clawed at his back as he entangled his fingers in her hair. She wrapped a bare leg around his hip, gliding herself up and down his thick thigh and coating her juices over him as he toyed with her nipples. They couldn't get enough of each other. Hands roamed feeling, exploring every inch of each other and setting nerves on fire and muscles to ache, screaming for release.

Toke dropped to his knees and lifted Revna's leg, placing her foot on his shoulder. He ran his tongue up her inner thigh in tantalisingly slow motions until Revna gripped his hair, letting him know she wanted him. Toke took the hint and slowly slid his long thick fingers inside her wetness, enjoying how her fingers pulled harder on his hair. He worked up a rhythm, and as her moans increased, he pushed a second and third finger inside. He could feel her legs shaking against him; seeing her turn weak at his touch pleased him. He could smell her arousal and wondered if she tasted as sweet as she smelt.

"Toke…" She panted, her free hand massaging her breast as Toke flicked his tongue over her aching bud, and his fingers continued their mission.

"Toke…." Revna moaned, her hands reaching up and taking hold of a branch to steady herself.

Toke loved the sound of his name on her tongue in the cries of ecstasy, but he wanted her to scream louder. To feel her release around him.

"I'm close…. I'm….oh, Toke," she panted before Toke sucked the sensitive bud between his teeth, finally sending her over the edge.

Revna reached down with one hand holding Toke's face firmly between her thighs as she rode out the end of her climax, her cries of ecstasy filling the space around them as she screamed his name. He allowed her leg to drop to the floor so she could steady herself. Then, he stood in front of her, admiring her post-climax face as she slowly came back to earth.

When she finally opened her eyes, she could see the remains of her pleasure on his lips. She wrapped her hand around his neck and pulled him to her, sucking on his bottom lip and licking the remains of herself off him.

Toke was surprised at how turned on he was by her brazenness, he wouldn't change her for the world. She let her lips wander down his neck, collar bone, and chest before teasing his nipples the same way he had with her. He tried to hide his moans of pleasure, keeping them trapped in the back of his throat, but she heard them. And she was living for it. Her kiss trailed further down his torso until she was on her knees.

Toke's cock was long and thick in her hand; she stroked half his length while resting in her mouth and rolling her tongue around him. Slowly she picked up speed, and evenly slowed; she took him deeper and deeper until he could feel the back of her throat. Then, finally, her hand slipped under to cup him, sending his eyes rolling with the onslaught of sensations.

"Revna....Odin's beard...oh Revna," he groaned.

She could taste the sweet saltiness as his pleasure grew; she knew he had to be close. She increased her speed, stroking with her hand, mouth, and tongue in a marvellous display of lust and primal animal desire.

"Revna!" he cried out. His pleasure exploded in her mouth.

His hips bucked, and he struggled to stay standing as his knees shook while his climax ripped through him, making him see stars.

"Impressive; any other man would be limp by now," Revna's voice purred in his ear as her eyes wandered back down to admire the beautiful muscle.

Toke opened his eyes as she licked her lips; she craved more. So did he.

"I've waited years to tell you how I feel, even longer to feel you. I'm not nearly through with you yet," he growled.

Wrapping his arms around her waist, he lifted her and pushed her back into the tree. Revna wrapped her arms around his neck and her hips around his waist. Toke was aware of his size and didn't want to hurt her. Slowly, he pushed himself into her, her moans of pleasure making him grow harder.

"All of you, Toke. I want to feel all of you," she panted.

Toke obliged; slowly, he slid all of him inside her and almost came undone again as he felt her clench around him.

"Fuck, Revna...." He groaned against her neck as she began to shake from his even strokes, he was making it last as long as possible.

Revna revelled in the feel of him. He filled every inch of her like he was made for her and only her. Nothing she had ever felt compared to Toke inside of her.

"Fuck me, Toke....hard," she purred, nipping at his ear.

He didn't need to be told twice. He pulled back, so only the tip of his cock remained inside her before slamming the length of him back in. Enjoying her cries of yes and screams of pleasure. He repeated the motion several times before he quickened his pace, her firm breasts bouncing in his face and the sweet sound of their bodies colliding echoing up the hill.

"Toke... I'm....Oh, by the gods...." She cried as she came apart around him again. It felt even better the second time around because he could feel her pulling him closer, taking all of him. He could feel her climax, and it brought on his own. Then, he spilt himself with a scream of her name and three more sharp, fast strokes. Panting for air as he slowly came back to reality.

EPILOGUE

Toke and Revna bathed quickly in the stream on their journey back into town. They met the others outside the inn, packed and ready for the next part of their expedition.

Thyra led them through the woods and back through the path leading northeast to the Point. The group pretended not to notice the change between Revna and Toke. However, it was glaringly obvious to everyone that they had settled their differences and finally admitted they had feelings for each other.

Revna and Toke rode side by side, mumbling over to each other like children. Occasionally, he would reach out and stroke her face. And in return, she would reach out and stroke the muscle between his legs, chuckling to herself when he would blush and pull his horse a little further away, worried Sven and the others might see her wandering hands.

"So, who do we think our new enemy is? Did they wear any identifying sigils?" Thyra asked when she noticed Sven kept glancing in Revna and Toke's direction.

"None. Before they attacked, they could easily be mistaken for hunters or maybe farmers," Revna answered.

"Except they were much too skilled for that," Toke said.

"Lord Beacham once worked with the Jarl. They gathered a local village and used them as a small army." Thyra informed them. "Do you think the Brits are up to their old tricks again?"

"It would make sense. The Jarl left word with someone about his treasure. But, of course, they will have expected to be paid. It takes many coins to arm and trains new soldiers. So the Brits are a real possibility," Lief said roughly, his face stern and deep in thought.

"Is someone about to declare war on the King? On Denmark?" Ulf asked.

No one answered, not wanting to speak their doubts or concerns, lest the gods hear.

"What if someone found out and just took it? Theft is common between the poorer classes, correct?" Arne ventured.

It was a much more straightforward answer, but they couldn't rule out the possibility of war, even if they wanted to.

"There are many questions and many answers. So let us pray to Odin that the next part of our journey gives us the answers we seek," Lief said thoughtfully.

THE END

COLINE

WORSHIPPED BY A VIKING

PROLOGUE

As Leif and his crew prepared to leave the inn to travel to the Point, a thought peeked into Lief's mind. A thought he couldn't shake. Noticing how Toke and Revna were preoccupied, as were Sven and their guide Thyra, Lief took the opportunity to pull Arne and Ulf aside. He didn't want his words to fall on Thyra's ears, knowing that her loyalty was to the Jürgensen brothers and the settlement.

"Are you confident you can find your way back to the Scottish settlement without Thyra's help?" he asked.

"Come now, Lief, look who you are talking to. We are not so distracted by the ways of women like our brothers here. Of course, we can find the settlement," joked Ulf.

Lief looked back at Ulf with a grave expression. This was no time for light-heartedness or fun. They had a mission to complete. And now that a new enemy had presented itself, time was of the essence.

"What grieves you?" Arne asked.

"The attack in the caves circles my mind. We are no longer the only ones hunting the Jarl's loot. Our mission must face no more delays, and we cannot afford others getting wind of our plans." Lief began, speaking in hushed tones, letting his eyes wander the inn for listening ears and watching eyes.

"We must find out who our new enemy belongs to, be them English or Highlander. Once we know our enemy, we will know how to defeat them. I wonder if anyone back at the settlement may have noticed clusters of armed men. Sören is strict with his scouting; if anyone knows, it will be him," Lief explained.

"Shall we warn Sören of the potential for war?" Arne enquired.

Lief kept quiet, hesitating. He rolled over Arne's question. The settlement was still a Danish settlement, be it on English shores or not. But Lief didn't trust easily, and he didn't know who he could trust in these strange lands. Word had reached his ears of how the brothers entrusted with running the settlement had married local women. Did their loyalties now lie with the enemy, or were their hearts still true to Denmark?

"No. Until we unmask our attackers, everyone who is not part of our group is an enemy. Be they English, Highlander, or Dane," Lief declared.

"Guilty until proven innocent. I like it," Ulf grinned.

"Keep your ears and eyes open. Find out as much as you can about the inhabitants of these lands and our Danish cousins. No matter how small the detail, anything may prove to be the key to protecting Denmark and the King," Lief instructed, as he mounted his horse.

"What will you tell the others of our departure?" Arne asked.

"Leave the others to me. Now go. Serve me well and serve your King even better," Lief nodded.

"Commander," Ulf and Arne said in unison, mounting their horses and leaving the group, heading back to the Scottish settlement.

CHAPTER 1

COLINE WAS JUST TRYING to keep her head down and do her chores. Her older sister, Sima, and her husband left for Beecham Castle to oversee the rebuild after the fire, leaving Coline, her mother, and brothers behind. Her brother-in-law had instructed that they be treated well in their absence. Highlanders among Vikings. They were not at war, but it didn't always feel peaceful either. Coline had been subjected to bullying and ridicule without Abjörn or Sima around to protect her. She was used to being judged by the Ladies of the King's court for being the second daughter - the *spare* - as they called her, and not the heir. But she had never experienced life like this. Name-calling and disapproving looks, she could cope with. She was witty, and Sima had taught her how to handle the court Ladies. But no one had prepared her for Viking bullying.

Coline had never been disillusioned by her father's wicked behaviour. Sima, being the eldest, always had a special bond with him. And since Lord Beecham had always wanted sons, when Coline's younger brothers came along, she was cast aside. The spare. That made no difference, as being Lord Beecham's offspring, she was disliked by the Vikings. She couldn't blame them, but she had given up trying to fight her case and that of her family. Now she wanted a simple life, an easy life.

Today's task was to fetch water for her mother to cook dinner with.

She had walked through the settlement many a time and found a path to the well that would allow her to pass unnoticed. Coline thought that she had managed until she snuck back towards the hut that was assigned to her and her family.

Keeping her head down and eyes cast to the floor, she stopped as a group of girls surrounded her. Several of them, barely into their teens, all a good handful of years younger than Coline. Still, they were Vikings, and Coline didn't want any trouble. As none of them moved, Coline took a nervous step forward, testing to see if they would let her pass. At first, they allowed Coline space to breathe. But then they took turns knocking into her with each step. It was causing her to spill her water, and they laughed at her distress.

"I want no trouble, please just let me pass," she asked, her voice barely a whisper. She was too scared to even let them hear her voice.

All her request did was make the girls laugh more and push a little harder until every drop of her water had been spilled. But that was not enough. The tallest of the girls gave Coline a hard shove causing her to tumble into the dirt, soiling her dress. The girl's friends erupted into laughs as they all ran away.

Coline was past the point of crying. Her shoulders weighed heavy for a woman barely into womanhood. She didn't want this life; she wanted to go home. She reached for her bucket, but to her surprise, she wasn't the only one. Looking up, she saw a tall, muscular Viking, unlike any she had seen before. While most have long, thick beards, this man had a clean jawline. His hair was dark and thick, tied neatly into a knot on his head. Emerald green eyes looked down at her while taking her bucket and offering his hand.

"Are you alright?" he asked, his voice deep yet soft and smooth.

Coline kept her eyes cast low and barely offered a nod. She worried if she spoke of her bullies and they got in trouble, they would do much worse to her next time.

"Stupid children need to learn respect. We are Vikings; we are above such juvenile acts of unkindness," he offered. His anger at her situation surprised Coline, as did his elegance with words.

Who was this man? Had her brother-in-law sent him to take care of her in his absence? If he had not, what would happen to her if she no longer had her brother-in-law's protection? Fear prickled her skin and made her throat dry.

"May I have my bucket back?" she asked, keeping her eyes cast down on the morsels of dirt, she brushed off her dress.

"Allow me to help you fill it and carry it back to your dwelling."

"Why would you do that?" she asked, noticeable panic in her voice.

Her mind raced with possibilities of what this handsome stranger could have planned for her. None of them were pleasant. Did he intend to harm her? Rape her? Get his revenge for the acts of her father? Now terrified by her thoughts, she glanced at him, her eyes landing on his. She didn't give him a chance to answer before she tried to flee.

Coline didn't get far before the strange Viking caught up to her in two quick strides with his tree trunk-sized legs. He wrapped his arms around her, pulling her back to him. With her back to his chest and his muscular biceps wrapped around her shoulders, Coline realised that she liked how she felt in his embrace. For the first time since arriving to the settlement, Coline felt somewhat safe. It was an unsettling feeling that she didn't know what to do with.

"You need not be afraid of me. My name is Arne; I mean you no ill will. Allow me to help you," his words brushed across her ear, causing the skin around her neck to prickle in a way she had never felt before. The hairs on the back of her neck stood on end, and her body responded on its own, relaxing back into him.

Coline didn't understand why she felt this way or how her body could respond of its own accord. She was scared both by the unknowing of this man and by the strange feelings intoxicating her blood. She felt she might cry. Near tears, hands trembling, and heart-pounding, she reacted the only way she knew how. A trick she had learned from her older sister.

"Leave me alone!" she yelled as she slammed the heel of her boot down as hard as she could onto Arne's toes.

The force caused his grip to loosen and his strong stance to waver. He didn't cry out as she had expected, but with his grip no longer as tight, she ducked out of his embrace and ran. She ran with everything she had, holding her skirts almost to her knees, not once looking back.

CHAPTER 2

"HA! HA! HA!" Ulf roared, laughing so hard that he held his side, and a stray tear escaped his eye. "Wait till the others hear of this, the great Arne, bested by a girl woman barely from childhood. I wonder if she has ever felt the warmth of a man, yet she bested you, with a mere foot stomp no less."

Arne stood his arms crossed over his chest, his brow furrowed deep, waiting for his closest friend to stop laughing. Arne didn't see what was so funny. She hadn't bested him. He had let her go, didn't he?

"You great oaf, this tale will be sung about for years. The great Arne allowed a woman to flee...." Ulf began to sing.

Ulf didn't have the best singing voice, but that wasn't why Arne interrupted him. Arne was confused by his words.

"Care to explain why *I* am the oaf, brother?" Arne asked, trying to keep the annoyance out of his tone.

"Did you not see her flaming red hair? She is a Highlander, most likely a slave. Why else would the children taunt her?"

Arne hadn't noticed her hair. All he had noticed was the sadness in her eyes. Those beautiful green eyes almost matched his. He hadn't noticed her hair, but he had seen the timidness of her movements and the fear that wafted from her presence, he could practically smell it. That's when he realised something.

Ulf stopped laughing as he, too, shared in Arne's thoughts. The friends stared at each other, realising what Ulf had just said. How had they not thought of it sooner? They had already spoken with Sören and his brother, to no avail. The brothers informed Ulf and Arne that they knew nothing of raiders or bandits around. That area was free and calm. Nothing unusual or untoward had been noted. Yet a Highlander walked among them. She could be a slave or a lover to one of the Danes, and if anyone knew of the rumours of the settlement, it would be her. She was obviously scared. But if asked in the right way, she could willingly give up what information she knew. Her knowledge could prove invaluable. Enemies of the Vikings, raiders, and bandits. The possibilities were endless.

ULF STOPPED A TALL, robust woman carrying a basket back from the market. She didn't seem happy to be stopped while on her errand, and Ulf took note of the impressive blade hanging from her hip.

"Excuse me, the red-haired girl?" Ulf asked, pointing off into the direction Coline had run, "she is a … Highlander, yes? Who owns her?"

"Owns her?" the woman coughed, "No one owns her."

Arne and Ulf shared another look. The woman clearly disapproved of the Highlander more than the children who had taunted her.

"She was a prisoner, and so was the rest of her family. They were set free," she continued.

"Set free? Why?" Arne asked.

"Ha! That's the question. I heard it was deemed that the family was spared, as the father had committed the crimes, not the wife and children. Ridiculous, if you ask me. Her sister has proven her loyalty. But who is to say the rest share her nature?" The woman snarled. No love was lost between her and the Beechams.

"Her sister? Who is the girl?" Arne asked.

The woman looked back, confused. How did they not know? Before answering their query, she looked at Arne and Ulf from head to toe.

"She is Lord Beecham's daughter, sister of Sima, who is the wife of

Abjörn. Surely you know who *he* is." She grunted before turning and continuing on her journey.

Wife of Abjörn? She is the sister-in-law of the oldest Jürgensen. That was why she didn't cringe at the sight of him. The thought jumped out and slapped him. Arne turned to Ulf and realised he had not been listening to the conversation.

"You know, Arne, the Highlander didn't exactly protest being held initially. If I didn't know any better, I'd say she liked the feel of your embrace," Ulf offered.

Arne thought back to how she felt in his arms and realised his brother spoke the truth. He remembered how she had relaxed into him, how as he gave her his name, her neck had tilted ever so slightly.

"If she is a free woman, then she can be seduced. A woman tells her lover things that she would say to no one else. If she is fearful for her life and her family's, she would likely tell a lover anything to help them. She would know of plots, gossip from the settlement, and information on the English King's court. She is Beecham's daughter. Her knowledge is what we need to complete our mission." Ulf offered, getting more excited with every word, obviously proud of his own conclusion.

"What are you saying?" Arne asked, cocking an eyebrow as the suspiciously happy look Ulf shot his way.

"She may have never felt the warmth of a man; she is scared. Make her feel safe. Seduce her, then get the information we need," Ulf answered.

Arne couldn't deny that it was a good plan. A foolproof one that might end with only an enemy getting hurt. But Arne had only ever been with a morsel of women. He did not have the charm and charisma of his friends. And he wasn't sure he liked being the one chosen to deceive someone so young and innocent.

"I know nothing of seduction," he admitted.

Ulf grinned, his eyes glowing with mischief and mayhem, "I will teach you."

CHAPTER 3

COLINE SAT on the floor by the large black iron pot, preparing dinner. Yet again, her mother had an excuse not to make dinner. Today's reason was a headache.

"It is not the job of the Lord's Lady to cook. That is what servants are for," she had complained.

"We are no longer in Beecham Castle, mother. We no longer have servants. How else are we supposed to eat if we do not cook it ourselves?"

"I have a headache from all these petty disagreements. I must go lay down."

Rolling her eyes, Coline picked up the vegetables and began to peel them. She knew how to prepare and cook food. While her father had taken Sima to court, preparing her for the day that she would take over as Lady of the castle, and her mother doted on her younger brothers, Coline had spent time with the servants. They were lovely people, and Coline hated how her mother treated them. She remembered spending many a day in the kitchens, preparing dinner and watching as they cooked. It was a secret that she was proud to keep to herself. Unlike her mother, Coline could care for herself and her family.

Peeling potatoes and carrots, Coline allowed her mind to wander as she smiled to herself, remembering how Cook had been so kind to her and how she would laugh and joke with her about her mother. She thought of how the woman had taught her things that her mother never would. Her reminiscing was interrupted by a knock at the door.

"Come in," Coline yelled, assuming it was one of the brothers, either Sören or Dittmer, the only ones to call on her.

"Good, I'm not too late and still of use," came a deep velvety voice that had Coline's skin erupting into goosebumps.

That same voice she had felt brush against her ear. The voice that had her body responding despite her mind. She turned to see the Viking....Arne, if she remembered rightly, was standing just inside her doorway. There was a bucket full of water in one hand and a small, hand-picked bunch of flowers in the other, a few stray roots still attached to the stems.

"What....how...." Coline stuttered.

How had he found her? What was he doing here? She didn't feel as scared as she had when they first met. She might be young and not the strongest, but she did hold a knife in her hand, and she had a way to keep herself safe.

"I felt awful that you had travelled to the well for nothing. I did offer my help before, but since you ran off so quickly, you left your bucket behind. I thought it might be needed." He said, stepping closer to her and placing the bucket by the pot.

"And the flowers?" Coline asked, startling herself.

Why had she asked? Where had the confidence come from? And why did her heart flutter as he handed them to her?

"An apology...for scaring you earlier. It was not my intention. I sometimes forget that I need to be gentle," Arne smirked.

Coline nervously took the flowers from his hand, never letting her suspicious gaze drop from his face. She wanted to watch for any signs of ill will. Uncomfortable under her stern, watchful gaze, Arne let his eye drift around the hut she called home. While he looked away, Coline brought the flowers to her nose and smiled at the smell. Her smile fading when she realised he was watching her, smiling back.

"This is a lovely hut you have. Do you live alone?" Arne ventured.

"I live with my brothers, whom you would have passed playing outside. And my mother is clearly on the cot in the corner," Coline answered, getting back to chopping her vegetables.

"Oh yes, I see that now," Arne answered, lost for words.

"You are not very good at small talk, are you? Why are you here?" She asked, ignoring the shaking of her hands as she struggled to keep the blade steady.

Arne opened his mouth to answer but didn't get a chance. A scream from outside startled him; before he could react, Coline was on her feet and pushing past him. Arne followed her outside and found the cry had come from one of her younger brothers. A boy no older than five years. He had fallen while playing, and his knee had a small cut, encrusted with mud and rocks. Tears streamed down his face as he clung to his knee.

Arne relaxed, seeing that there was no threat of danger and that no one was truly hurt. He watched as Coline scooped the boy into her arms and rocked him, trying to calm his cries. Arne walked over to join them, kneeling in front of her and lifting the boy's chin with his thumb so the boy looked him in the eyes.

"Vikings do not cry when we fall. We get back up, and we fight," Arne said.

Coline's brow furrowed, her suspicious gaze glaring back at him as her grip on her brother tightened.

"I am not a Viking," the boy squeaked.

"Do you not live in a Viking hut? In a Viking settlement? Is your older sister not married to a mighty Viking?"

The boy's cries softened, and he nodded gently back at him.

"Then you, my boy, are a Viking. Are you strong? Are you brave? Can you fight with a sword and ride a horse?"

"Yes, I am strong. Yes, I am brave. I fight with sticks and ride my pony," The boy replied, whipping his tears on his sleeve.

"Then, my boy, you are a Viking." Arne smiled at him.

"Let me tell you a secret. But you must promise not to tell anyone. Only Vikings know this," Arne whispered, beckoning the boy closer, glancing around as though he were checking for spies.

"I want to know too," chirped his brother.

"Then come," Arne said.

The two boys ran towards Arne, huddled close to hear his big secret.

"Us Vikings cry. We are not afraid to cry. But we do it when we are in private, hidden from the world."

"Why?" asked the eldest of the boys.

"Because that way, the world does not see our fear, our love. When we are hurt, we stand up and show the world that we are the fiercest, strongest warriors. We attack the world, letting it know that it cannot hurt us. It can only hurt us if we let it." Arne stopped letting his eyes fall to Coline, who watched him closely.

"Can I trust you with the secret, boys?"

Both boys stood firm and nodded their heads vigorously.

"Good, now, come. Grab your fighting sticks and let me show you how Vikings fight."

The boys cheered and danced around the yard, each jabbing sticks at Arne, who mocked injury and death as the boys lunged and jabbed at him. Coline couldn't help but smile; it was a sight for sore eyes, for a fearsome warrior, a man built like a bear. He was soft and kind and excellent with children. It was an odd mix, and Coline didn't know what to make of him. Was he genuine? Was it all an act? She didn't know whom she could trust anymore, and the more she watched Arne play with her brothers, the more she realised that she couldn't trust herself either.

Her heart fluttered at his straining muscles; her stomach flipped every time his eyes locked with hers. Her mind told her to be cautious; her heart told her to stay away. But her body screamed out for him.

"Coline, look! We bested a Viking. A mighty Viking," cheered her younger brother, snapping her out of her darkening thoughts.

"Yes, George, that you did," she smiled.

"Coline! So nice to finally know your name." Arne grinned as he rose to his feet.

He stepped closer to her, towering over her, forcing her to crane her neck back to look up at him. He stood so close, yet not close enough to touch. She wanted to reach out and touch him, but she didn't know why. She was drawn to him; it was curious.

"I must carry on cooking dinner, if you would excuse me," said Coline, dipping into a low courtesy before hurrying inside.

She was glad to get away, scooping bowls of water out of the bucket to cover the vegetables. She could still hear Arne playing with the boys outside, but she needed space to think and had tasks to keep her hands and mind busy.

CHAPTER 4

COLINE AWOKE the next morning to the sound of an axe connecting with wood. Confused, she swiftly dressed and checked on her mother and brothers. None of them seemed to be startled by the noise as they all slept soundly huddled up in one big blanket.

Coline headed outside and found the cow had already been milked. A full pail sat on the doorstep waiting for her. She ventured further into the yard, following the noise. That's when she saw it. Him. Arne. Standing shirtless, sweat dripping down his iron-clad chest as he chopped firewood. Coline watched as he brought the axe high over his head and sliced a piece of wood, as long and thick as a small tree, in half with one hard swing. Her pulse raced, and she gulped for air as she watched him take the two halves and split them again. And again.

Thankfully, he hadn't noticed her watching. He stopped and wiped the sweat from his brow with the back of his hand, turning to get a drink of water from the pail behind him. Coline was filled with a sudden flush of anger and frustration, feeling more confident than she had since she was first brought to the settlement. She stormed across the yard from her hiding place to demand answers.

"What on earth do you think you are doing?" she demanded.

"Good morning, my Lady," Arne winked, taking another sip of water from the small wooden bowl.

"Don't call me that. You can't be doing things for me. What will people think? That will get the wrong idea. You must go, and in the name of the heavens, put on some clothes." Coline protested, turning away so he couldn't see her cheeks blush as he tensed his chest muscles, making his pectorals dance before her eyes.

"And what exactly is the wrong idea?"

"Well….They will think you are interested in me, for one thing," Coline answered, keeping her back to him.

She heard his footsteps as he drew closer. She held her stance as he moved around to stand in front of her, once again forcing her to look up at him. However, this time, she found that she had a more challenging time not letting her eyes drift as his chest heaved in front of her.

"That would be bad because?" Arne ventured.

"I am Lord Beecham's, daughter. In the English court, it is wrong for a man to be seen attempting to court a woman who has not been promised to him. Also, my family is hated here. If people see, they will think I am trying to seduce you, to gain favour, to…to…." She grew more frustrated with all the reasons she could think of, but the more his eyes burned into hers, the more she found she was lost for words.

She tried to speak again, but her words caught in her throat as Arne scooped his hand around the back of her neck and one around her waist, pulling him into her before he lay a kiss on her lips. He kissed her hard and fast, surprised when he felt that she did not attempt to stop him. But she did not attempt to kiss him back. Gently, he let her go and watched as she stood bewildered, eyes still softly closed where he had left her. He waited until she regained herself and her eyes fluttered open.

"Perhaps…my Lady…it is you who has the wrong idea," Arne whispered in her ear, allowing his fingers to gently stroke her neck as he brushed a few strands of her fiery red hair out of the way.

Stepping back, he grinned. He was satisfied, looking at her in her flustered state of shock. With another wink and a smirk, he began to whistle a tune Coline didn't know as he turned away from her and began stacking the freshly chopped wood.

Coline was utterly perplexed. *What just happened?* She asked herself as once again she stood frozen watching Arne and his muscles dance as he worked the firewood.

CHAPTER 5

LATER THAT DAY, Coline decided that she needed some time away from the settlement. She decided to head up the hillside where she knew of a good bush where berries grow. As she walked through the settlement with her basket in hand, she couldn't help but notice how everyone gave her a wide birth once again. Even the girls who once taunted her were leaving her alone. It reminded her of how people avoided her when her brother-in-law still resided in the settlement. They left her alone and did not taunt or tease, though still not being friendly with her. She smiled at passers-by who looked at her, seemingly offended by her politeness. Sighing and letting her shoulders sag, she cast her eyes back to the floor and walked out of the settlement.

Why does my life have to be so complicated?

As she walked up the hill, she thought over the day's events and how things appeared to change the moment Arne showed up and interrupted the girls bullying her. *This is all his doing; I warned him what others would think*, Coline argued with herself. *Why can't he leave me alone?*

She passed a section of trees and rounded the berry bushes, out of sight from the settlement. Daydreaming, she half expected to bump into him. And Arne did not disappoint.

"Well, fancy seeing you here," Arne teased, plucking a berry from the bush and popping it into his mouth.

"You need to leave me alone. Please, just go." Coline pleaded.

"Why? Why must I go? It is clear that we like each other, right?" Arne asked, taking a step closer to her.

"I have no interest in you, and I have nothing to offer you."

"Oh, I doubt that, my Lady," Arne whispered as he grazed her cheek gently with his thumb. "I remember how you sank into me the first time we met."

"I do not know what you mean," Coline breathed.

Arne slinked around her and wrapped his arms around her shoulders like he had when she tried to flee. Once again, Coline sank into his embrace. Something about him called to her; was it his scent? His charm? Or those mystic emerald eyes?

"Tell me you do not like it when I touch you like this," Arne began as he trailed kisses down her neck.

Coline tried her hardest not to respond when her body cried out for his touch. She wanted to tilt her neck more, to give him better access, but she told herself to remain still.

"Tell me you don't like it when I do this," Arne continued as he slid the fabric off her shoulder, his trail of kisses travelling from her ear down her neck, collar bone, and shoulder. Coline couldn't help it. She shivered at his touch, and a small groan of pleasure escaped her lips.

"If you tell me that you don't like it. I will stop....." He nipped at her neck while his other hand slid into her bodice, and his fingers traced the delicate skin around her nipples. "Tell me to stop," he whispered in her ear.

Coline had been brought up with the belief that lying was wrong. A sin. So, she couldn't tell Arne that she didn't like the feel of his touch because that would be a lie. She couldn't tell him she wanted him to stop because she didn't. She wanted more. Her breathing picked up pace as Arne's hand slid further into her bodice; she fought back moans of pleasure as he tweaked the aching flesh of her breasts. She felt her hands moving of their own accord, stroking up his thighs as she leaned against him. She reached around and could feel how aroused he was by her too. At her touch, Arne let out a groan in her ear.

Arne slid his other hand down and gathered her skirt, pulling it up enough so he could feel the muscles beneath. His hand stroked her flesh, travelling up her thigh until it reached the centre of her being. His fingers spread her apart, rubbing the throbbing bud between her legs, making Coline's knees tremble.

"No!" Coline yelled, pushing his hands off her and jumping out of his embrace.

Tugging at her clothes, she straightened herself up and wrapped her arms around herself defensively.

"Did I hurt you?" Arne panicked.

"No, no, not at all. It's just that we do not know anything about one another. We can't do this without knowing each other. It's wrong." Coline protested.

Arne grinned at her, stepping closer. Coline took a step back with every step forward until she was cornered between Arne and a tree. Once again, he came back to lay kisses down her neck, letting his hands tease her and travel up and down her body.

"So, tell me. Tell me everything about you, Coline. I want to know," Arne breathed.

"What do you....What..." Coline gasped as his hands found the sweetness between her legs.

"Tell me about your family. Tell me about your friends. I know you are a Highlander; are there more of you, or are you alone?" Arne asked, his kisses travelling down as he pulled a breast free of her clothes, taking it into his mouth and making Coline groan.

"Wait. What did you say?" Coline asked, her mind ringing with alarm bells.

Something was off with his line of questioning; it was odd and not what one would expect when trying to get to know someone you intend to court.

"I asked if you are alone here in the settlement or if there are more Highlanders with you," Arne answered, lost in his task of getting to know all the places on Coline that made her weak.

"Get off me!" Coline yelled, shoving Arne as hard as she could.

It wasn't very hard, and Arne was a strong man. But her words carried more weight with him than her fists. He did as he was told and stepped back, giving her space, not wanting to scare or hurt her.

"Of all the questions you could have asked me, why that one? What are you hiding?" She demanded,

"I am hiding nothing," Arne answered.

"Liar! I demand to know what you are doing here, with me!" Coline yelled, her anger plain to see on her face and in her voice.

"I apologize, my Lady...."

"Don't call me that."

"I am sorry, Coline." Not wanting to be caught in a lie, he continued, "I may have been trying to seduce you to find out what you know about Highlanders and other English plots," Arne answered, bowing his head.

Guilt plagued him. This may have started as a fact-finding mission, and his intentions may have once been unpure. But he never meant to hurt the girl. He was a better man than that; how had he allowed himself to become so toxic? And now he wanted nothing more than to hold her close.

"So, all of this was a lie?" Coline snapped, her voice catching in her throat.

"It may have been that way at first, but I see you. I want to know more. And not just about these strange lands. Let me know you," Arne pleaded, reaching out his hands.

Hurt, betrayed, furious, yet still quite aroused, Coline suddenly realised how her clothes still hung off her, how her breasts were still exposed to him. Pulling herself together, she ignored the stirring in her belly, the ache between her legs, and the pain in her heart. Anger took hold. The more she looked at his face, the darker a hatred inside her grew. Without thinking, Coline grabbed her bucket of berries and tossed it with all her might at Arne's head.

She didn't wait around to see if it hit its intended target, but she knew it had by the yell she heard as she stormed off back down the hill towards the settlement.

CHAPTER 6

Rubbing the new bump on his head and carrying Coline's basket, Arne walked back to the settlement. Kicking himself. *Well, I royally made a mess of that, didn't I?* Frustrated and mumbling to himself, he headed out to find Ulf; perhaps his friend could offer some advice.

Ulf had been out with Sören and his scouts all day, returning just as Arne entered the settlement.

"What in Odin's beard happened to you?" Ulf asked, dismounting, and letting the scout take the horseback to the stables.

"I messed up."

"How?"

Arne sighed and tossed the basket to the side, letting it roll by the settlement's gates. Still rubbing his head, he told Ulf everything that had happened between him and Coline. It didn't take long before Ulf again burst out into belly-rolling laughter.

"You are an idiot. How hard is it to bed a woman? You have bedded a woman before, haven't you?" Ulf roared.

"Of course I have. It's not simply about bedding a woman. I like her; she is sweet and not like anyone I have met before. I want the chance to get to know her, not just bed her and run."

"Oh, in the name of Thor, don't go getting soft on me too. It's bad enough with Toke and Sven," Ulf groaned.

"Don't mock me, Ulf. Besides, I don't think she has anything to do with any plots or even knows of anything of worth. She is frightened of her own shadow; she won't risk being caught up in a mess like this. Besides, her family seems to be the centre of her world; she wouldn't risk putting them in danger." Arne argued.

"You have been out with the scouts all day. What did you find?" Arne asked, trying to shift the spotlight onto something other than himself and the feelings he admitted aloud before analysing them himself.

Ulf shook his head and kicked at a loose rock. "Nothing. Sören was right; nothing is a miss. Perhaps we are worried over nothing. The attack in the cave may have been a fluke. Men from the inn trying their luck maybe."

"Perhaps you are right. We shall leave in the morning. Go back and try and catch up with the other. Leave this sorry mess behind," Arne said, clapping his friend around the back.

"I think you are right. Tonight, we feast, rest, and then we ride in the morning," Ulf cheered.

The sound of pounding hooves had the friends turning to the gates. An errand boy on horseback, face awash in panic and sweat dripping from him, gasped for breath as his horse pulled to a stop.

"What is it, boy?" asked one of Sören's scouts who had run up behind Ulf and Arne without them realising.

"It is Sima and Abjörn. Beecham Castle is under attack," panted the young boy.

Arne caught the flashes of something, someone, moving near one of the huts by the gate. Turning out of the corner of his eye, he saw Coline. She had heard everything. Her face flushed, her eyes were wide in horror, and her mouth hung open. Arne expected her to run, and she did, just not where he expected.

Arne thought she might run home, away from him and his betrayal. Instead, she ran out of the settlement and through the trees the same way the errand boy had come. She ran towards her family. She ran towards Beecham Castle.

CHAPTER 7

ARNE GRABBED the raise of a horse one of the scouts walked his way. He mounted and took off after Coline, ignoring the scout and Ulf's screams after him. Given she was on foot and he was on horseback, it didn't take long for him to catch up to her. Jumping off the horse, he ran to her grabbing her, wanting to calm her panicked mind, and keep her safe. Battle was no place for a Lady of the court. A trained sword or shieldmaiden, yes, but not a Lady of the court, especially not one so young as Coline.

Coline fought hard against Arne's embrace, crying hysterically. Her fight impressed Arne. She was fiercer than he expected, given how frightened she seemed by the world around her.

"Let me go! I must get to Sima. Sima needs me," she cried.

"Calm down, Coline; battle is no place for one so young. Her husband will not let anything happen to her. I have heard of his escapades. He is a force to be reckoned with. Your sister will be safe," Arne tried to reassure her, but all Coline did was fight against him, trying to break free.

"She wasn't supposed to be there," Coline cried.

Her statement started something in Arne. He began to think. Maybe he was wrong about her, perhaps she had managed to fool him, and she did know more than she said. Anger and embarrassment pooled in his blood. He had allowed her to beat him once. His pride wouldn't allow it a second time.

Grabbing Coline by the shoulder, he pinned her against a tree. Holding her still, her eyes widened in fright at the anger in his eyes.

"You are allied with our enemies? Do you spy for them from inside the settlement? Tell me what you know! Do not lie to me!" Arne roared.

Coline froze, shocked by Arne's outburst. "I do not know what you are talking about," she protested.

"Who is attacking the castle?" Arne demand.

"I do not know!" Coline screamed back, tears brimming her eyes.

"You said she wasn't supposed to be there. You know something so tell me!" Arne roared.

Anger grew inside Coline, and anger she didn't know she was capable of. Standing her ground, she pushed back. Arne didn't move. But now he knew that she wasn't scared of him, or anything else anymore.

"It's Sima! My sister, you great blubbering fool. She wasn't supposed to go with Abjörn to assist with rebuilding the castle. She left last minute because she's too head over heels in love with him to leave his side. That's what I was upset about! *I could lose my sister*! The only person who has ever truly cared for me in this world!" Coline screamed.

"Does my answer satisfy you? Oh, mighty Viking?" She screamed in his face.

Arne didn't move. He stood staring, trying to size Coline up to see if she was telling the truth.

"Here is something my sister taught me," Coline snarled. Directing all her fury at Arne, she brought her knee to his groin with all the anger and force she could muster.

Arne crumpled to the floor, grabbing at his crotch. To his surprise, she had a mean hit for such a small thing. Shoving Arne aside, she ran past him and jumped on his horse, leaving him in the dust as she raced off to help her sister.

CHAPTER 8

ULF CAUGHT up and witnessed the entire encounter. Arne glared at Ulf as he laughed uncontrollably. Arne was beginning to grow tired of his friend laughing at his expense.

"Will you quit laughing," Arne groaned, struggling to get to his feet as his crotch ached.

"I can't help it, brother. Look at the mess this woman has got you into," Ulf chuckled. "You failed to keep hold of her the first time, you failed to bed her, and now she knocks you on your backside and steels your horse. Are you sure you are a Viking?" Ulf teased.

"You are an idiot," Arne snapped.

"It is all in good fun, brother. Lighten up," Ulf spat back.

"It's always in good fun when it's at my expense. Did I laugh at you when...."

Ulf interrupted; he knew where Arne was going, and they had agreed never to speak of it again. "Hey now, that's not fair; we had an agreement never to speak of that battle again. Besides, my mistake was mine alone. I never let my judgment be clouded by a skirt, especially a Highlander skirt." Ulf complained.

Arne snapped, losing his temper. He grabbed Ulf, pulling him off his horse. The two friends stood nose to nose, tempers barely contained.

"Arne, what has gotten into you?" Ulf snapped, shoving Arne, but Arne didn't loosen his grip, holding Ulf fast.

"She is more than a skirt, and I will not have you talking about her that way. Do you understand me?"

"In the name of Thor and all of Asgärd, not you too." Ulf sneered. "What is it with these shores? All the men seem to be instantly bewitched."

"Enough, brother, before you step too far," Arne warned, shoving Ulf, finally letting go of his friend's collar.

"Too far? She is a means to an end; she is a Highlander and a source of information. Nothing more. Think clearly, you great oaf," Ulf snapped.

"She is more than that. She is like no woman I have ever met. She is...." Arne stopped as he noticed Ulf's face creasing. Ulf struggled to contain his laughter again.

"A man with a heart of stone like you will never understand. I'm taking your horse."

"Where do you intend to go?" Ulf asked.

"To save the woman I love before she gets herself killed."

"Love? Arne, be reasonable. You do not know the girl. She is barely into womanhood and...."

"I do not care for anything you have to say. There is no other word to describe how I feel about her. You do not need to understand it; you just need to accept it. You are my closest and oldest friend, Ulf. Think with reason, when have I displayed feelings such as this?" Arne declared as he mounted Ulf's horse.

Ulf stood watching. His face was serious for the first time since they arrived back at the settlement. He gave his friend a nod. Admitting defeat in their exchange and agreeing to support his friend.

"Ride after her; I will head back to the settlement and gather more forces. See you on the battlefield, my friend."

Arne nodded back, kicking the horse, spurring him on. Arne rode aimlessly into the woods, following the direction he last saw Coline riding his horse. He knew not of Beecham Castle's location, but as he drew deeper into the woods, the sounds of battle acted as his compass.

A small army battled to try and take the castle. Archers high on the hill loosed flaming arrows trying to cut off and divide the Viking forces. Despite the rain from the previous few days, the land by the castle was oddly dry; the flames ignited the walls surrounding the castle with ease.

Men on foot and horseback charged at Arne. Pulling his sword, he sliced through them with ease, his mind on one thing and one thing only. Finding Coline. A horse crying out in distress called his attention; it was a whine he knew well. His head snapped to the right to see Coline struggling to control his horse as it bucked her off and tried to flee from the flames. Turning in her direction, Arne prepared to ride when a wall of arrows spooked the horse he was set upon and he jumped off as it fled. Their archers were not so skilled against a moving target.

He was now reunited with his own steed. With enough time to calm the beast, he could no longer see Coline. Panic set in, she could be in danger, and he was outnumbered. Arne soon realised the archers were not aiming to hit him; they were meant as a distraction. And soon he was in the height of battle surrounded by horsemen brandishing swords, shields, and axes.

CHAPTER 9

ARNE WASN'T in the best position for battle. The surrounding area was thick with trees and uneven land. Being outnumbered, he needed a better vantage point to fight. Raising his sword, he swung and sliced the shoulder of the horse closest to him. He hated hurting animals, but if the horse couldn't run, neither could its rider. The horse bucked in pain, tossing its rider off its back. The man fell to the floor with a crash, and Arne charged his horse down the hill and passed the fallen rider to more stable ground.

As he rode to a safe clearing for battle, Arne leaned over the side of his horse, swinging his broad sword, slicing off limbs and cracking skulls. Fortunately, his attackers didn't seem as skilled as he; they struggled to follow him down the hill, their horses protesting against instruction and too scared to venture near the flames. Arne's horse was also scared of the fire, but the mighty beast knew it was safe with Arne. He had a way with horses.

"I will not let the flames touch you, my friend. Stay close, protect me, and I will protect you," he said, stroking the horse's neck as he dismounted.

The beast seemed to understand his words, bucking, and kicking at soldiers approaching. Whether out of fear of the flames or self-defence, Arne chose to believe the gods protected him and his steed as they fought as one.

Arne picked up a second sword from a fallen soldier. It wasn't as well-made as his, or as heavy, but it would serve its purpose. Arne battled for his life. He was no stranger to a fight and had secured many a victory in battle. But never before had Arne felt he was on the battle-field alone. Vastly outnumbered, he had to think fast. Twisting and turning, constantly changing his position to avoid predictability. Arne swung his swords, lopping off heads. Lunging, he ran men through, slicing stomachs and spilling guts. The harder he fought, the more his shoulders ached. Where were the others?

With his back turned, he heard a man approach with a war cry. Arne knew his time was up. He would be dining with his ances-tors in Valhalla before sundown. Arne made peace with his fate; pulling his sword free, he spun around to see a soldier almost as robust as he. Axe pulled high; a mighty blade made to kill. A blade that was almost as impressive as any Viking weaponry. Arne prepared to fight when the man tripped. A sign from the gods. Odin is not ready for me yet, he thought. Twisting his sword, Arne brought it down, impaling the man between his shoulder blades.

"Coline!?" Arne breathed, seeing what the man had fallen over.

She lay at his feet a broad sword far too big for her to handle. It didn't take long for Arne to piece the scene together. Coline had stolen the blade. It had been too heavy, and she had fallen, but not before taking the soldier's legs from under him first.

"I couldn't leave you. You needed help," she panted as Arne pulled her to her feet.

"This sword is far too big for you," Arne smiled, relieved to have her in his arms.

"It was all I could grab; I had to do something."

"We shall discuss this later. Take this; it is lighter. You may be able to handle it," Arne said, handing her the smaller sword and raising her up, putting her firmly on his horse's back.

Coline fought the best she could from up high, watching Arne's movements and matching them as men charged. Arne couldn't help but be impressed at her quick learning and bravery. She had come such a long way from the frightened girl he rescued from bullies only days before. *Did she learn to fight somewhere*? So little did he know about her past. So much to share when this was over.

Finally, a roar from over the hills sent fear through the men attacking Beecham Castle. The other Vikings from the settlement had arrived. The battle was won before it even began. Using the moment's distraction and fear in their eyes, Arne quickened his attacks. Ulf ran up, joining his friend, and they fought side by side until a horn signalled retreat, and the rest of the forces left. A cheer of Viking victory rang through the trees.

"You fought well," Ulf said reluctantly, nodding at Coline.

"Thank you," she answered, directing her attention to Arne rather than Ulf. "I must find my sister."

"She will most likely be inside; come, I will take you," Arne smiled.

The Vikings had protected the castle well. No man had made it past the front gates. Men ran with buckets full of water, dousing the flames and saving what they could regarding the restoration.

On entering Beecham Castle, Arne was stopped by two Vikings set to protect the door.

"State your business," one said.

"This is…." Arne began, interrupted by a surprised shriek.

"Coline? Let them pass; this is my sister," Sima yelled, running down the hall, embracing her sister and holding her tight.

"What on earth are you doing here? Are you hurt?" Sima asked, checking her sister over, alarmed at the dirt and blood that splattered her dress.

"I am fine, sister. I heard of the attack and knew I had to come and help you. I do not know what I would do in this world without you," Coline said, tears seeping from her eyes.

"You rode into battle?" Sima asked, surprised.

"She didn't just ride into battle. She saved my life," Arne bowed his head. "She fought well, my Lady."

Sima looked from Arne to Coline in complete surprise. Her eyes softened, and a smile spread across her lips. Coline and Sima were more alike than she had first realised.

"I'm so proud of you," Sima said, hooking her arm in her sister's and leading her through the halls.

CHAPTER 10

WITH THE CASTLE NOW SECURE, the Vikings assessed the damage and secured the castle before settling in for the night's feast. In the dining hall, everyone cheered, drank, and ate until their bellies were full. Sima and Abjörn headed the main table with Coline and Arne at their side. Sima occasionally passed Coline a knowing look. After the battle, Arne and Coline had been inseparable; Sima joked with her sister that Arne had taken to following her like a lost puppy.

Arne didn't want to leave Coline's side. While he had no doubt she was intelligent and brave, she was still such a small thing, and he had worried she could be killed. He didn't think twice about putting himself in the heat of battle to protect her, and he knew he would do it all over again in a heartbeat.

With Sima preoccupied with her husband and the attention of his brothers who had come over from the settlement, Arne took a moment to speak with Coline.

"You amaze me, my Lady."

"Why do you insist on calling me that?"

"Because you are a Lady and….my Lady," Arne winked. "You fought so bravely. If I had not seen it with my own eyes, I would not think of you as the same timid thing who spilled her bucket of water that day," Arne admired.

Coline said nothing; his words rendered her speechless.

"When I first laid eyes on you, you were scared of your own shadow. When that messenger road into camp and I saw you by the gates, I half expected you to run in fear, but you didn't; you ran towards danger. Your only thought was to protect your sister. I cornered you, accused you of being a traitor, and your mind was still on your family. Disregarding your own safety, you put me on my backside."

"Are you going somewhere with this?" Coline smirked.

"I'm proud of you, my Lady. I have had the honour of fighting with many a warrior, but none have ever surprised me like you."

"Thank you, your words mean a great deal," Coline blushed.

"I'm still mad at you."

"What for?" Coline asked in surprise.

"You ran into battle unarmed. You could have been killed, or worse, those men could have taken you and done the unspeakable," Arne answered, his genuine concern for her evident in his voice and sparkling from his eyes.

"If you recall, Arne, I did not need a weapon in battle," Coline sipped on her drink, enjoying Arne's look of confusion. "I took down a man almost as big as you with my body alone. I also took you down without a weapon, twice I might add. I am quite skilled in using my body as its own weapon. A skill I learned from Sima."

Arne sat straighter at her words. His body woke as his thoughts darkened, and his eyes reflected the lust stirring in his groin. Then, glancing around to make sure no one else was listening, he leaned in close to meet her eyes, running a finger up and down her thigh.

"I wonder what other skills your body has to lay a man down," Arne growled seductively in her ear.

Coline breathed in a deep breath and closed her eyes. He could feel her body responding to his touch and to the breath on her neck. Coline glanced around, everyone was deep in conversation, and the room had begun to empty as others made off to sleep for the night.

"I can show you....take me to your room," she whispered, taking his hand and rising from the table.

Arne and Coline rushed through the halls, the effects of the mead hitting them as soon as they rose to their feet. Laughing like children, they passed by other Vikings enjoying their evening. Opening the door to the room high in the castle assigned to Ulf and Arne for the evening, the pair fall silent when they saw Ulf lying on the cot in the far corner.

"Evening, brother," Arne smiled, pulling Coline closer to him and burying his face in her hair, causing her to chuckle. "Beautiful evening for a stroll, don't you think?"

"Be still, Arne. I can take a hint. I shall lay my head somewhere else this evening," Ulf groaned, rolling his eyes but offering Arne a wink as he left the pair to their privacy.

"Now, where were we?" Arne grinned, pulling Coline against him.

"I believe I was about to show you the other ways my body is skilled," Coline teased, pushing herself out of his embrace.

Coline took Arne and led him across the room, gently pushing him down to sit on the cot. With his eyes upon her, she stepped back and slowly began to pull apart the ties of her bodice. With her eyes glued to his, she teased him as she disrobed. Making every movement as slow as possible. She suppressed a satisfied grin as she watched his chest rise and fall as his breathing became heavier. Finally, she stood before him, the candlelight highlighting her long legs, the curves of her hips, and her subtle breasts. She slowly turned, giving Arne a view of her high, firm buttocks, her hands roaming softly over her breasts and down to the small patch of red hair between her legs.

Arne sat with his jaw open, mesmerised not just by the beauty that stood before him but the confidence that radiated off her like heat. The lust in her eyes, and how she subtly bit her bottom lip. He couldn't wait to clap that lip between his teeth. But she had done exactly what she said she would. She had rendered him useless. He wanted to jump up and ravish her, but he couldn't. His growing lust strained painfully under the restraints of his clothing, causing him to shift to make the pain ease.

"Here, let me help you," Coline breathed as she stepped forward, peeling his shirt from his shoulders.

She let out a small gasp at seeing the muscles of his shoulders bulging and the wall of muscle that was his chest. Her mind flashed back to the morning she watched him chopping firewood, and she felt herself grow damp. Kneeling between his legs, she pulled at his waistline. Arne tilted his hips, allowing her to free him. Her eyes fell on the muscle that twitched in anticipation, the thickness, and how it curved.

"Coline, may I ask you something?"

"You may."

"Have you ever lain with a man before?"

"Yes, but not one as....substantial as you," Coline answered, looking at him through her lashes.

Arne felt his mouth go dry at the way she looked at him. He pulled her up from her knees, and she sat astride him; he gripped her buttocks, spreading her wider as she lowered herself onto him. Arne gasped, feeling the gloriousness that was Coline as he filled her. Slowly adjusting to his size, Coline rocked her hips, pushing herself, raising, stroking his length.

Arne kept a firm hold of her backside, helping her keep the slow rhythm and pace she set. Coline wrapped her arms around his neck and pulled him into her, bringing her lips down on his, opening her mouth and tasting the remainders of the mead on his tongue.

Arne groaned against her lips, enjoying how she clenched herself around him as she began to pick up her pace. Then, taking her breasts in hand, just over a handful, Arne nipped at her flesh, rolling his tongue over her erect nipples, making her shudder and jolt on top of him.

Coline's soft moans grew into quickened pants that matched Arne's, as their pleasure built. The bud between Coline's legs ached, and waves of pleasure rolled through her. Coline arched her back and kept her pace, resting her hands on her lover's knees. Arne reached an arm around her waist to support her as he slipped his hand between her legs, circling her with his thumb.

"I want to feel you come apart around me," Arne breathed, his thumb matching Coline's pace.

Arne kept his eyes on her as her jaw fell open. Gasping at his touch, her moans grew louder, and she squeezed her eyes shut. Her hips bucked wildly, and her legs clamped hard around Arne's waist as her cries of ecstasy filled the room.

Coline collapsed against his chest, panting for air. Arne wrapped his arms around her, letting her catch her breath as her cave pulsed and constricted, sending waves of pleasure through him. Coline kissed his shoulder, and her hands roamed over his chest.

Keeping himself buried deep within her, Arne gently flipped their position and lay Coline down beneath him on the bed.

"You are a very talented woman," Arne breathed, laying kisses over her breasts. "Now it is my turn to make you weak."

Arne lay his body on top of Coline, entangling his fingers in her long red hair, his tongue massaging hers. Coline hooked her legs around his waist and ran her fingers through his hair. Arne teased her the way she had teased him, keeping his pace slow, pulling himself almost out before slamming himself deeply. The more Coline cried out in pleasure, the slower he went until he could feel his own pleasure brimming deep inside.

Arne pulled back and scooped Coline in his arms, flipping her onto her stomach. She rested her head on her arms as he arched her back and pulled her backside high. Pushing himself inside, he picked up his pace, taking her buttocks in his hands and kneading her. He wanted to hear her scream out one last time before he felt his release. Leaning forward as he slammed deeper and harder, he took a breast in one hand and reached under to stroke her between her legs. Coline ached and cried out his name, her voice echoing against the walls as they came apart together.

It wasn't enough, as they continued to wrap themselves around each other, enjoying every part of one another until the sun began to rise.

"My Lady," Arne whispered, kissing her softly on the forehead as she slept peacefully in his arms.

EPILOGUE

ARNE HID a yawn behind his hand; Ulf chuckled, knowing why his friend was so tired just after dawn. Together in the Lord's counsel chamber, Abjörn, Sören, Ryker, Ulf, and Arne gathered to discuss the attack. A new enemy presented itself. One they hadn't expected. They had spent so long trying to figure out who their enemy was. Little did they expect two of their enemies to join forces. The army that attacked Beecham Castle had been both British and Highlander.

It made no sense since there was no love between Brits and Highlanders, so why had they joined forces now? And what did they want from the Vikings?

"The enemy of my enemy is my friend," Ryker said.

"They can't work together for long; they will tear each other apart before they beat us," Sören said.

"Don't be foolish, brother. That attack was but a small show of force; we have no idea their size or strength. For enemies to have joined forces, they must have a common ground." Abjörn groaned, running his fingers through his beard.

"Yes, us," Ulf scoffed.

"Why join forces? Why attack us?" Sören asked.

Ulf and Arne shared a look, seemingly reading each other's minds. Then, with a nod, Ulf stepped forward.

"This isn't the first time they have joined forces. It makes sense to us now. Revna and Toke were attacked in a cave on the trail to the Point. They were almost killed. They couldn't identify their attackers. Now we know it is part of the same army that attacked last night," Ulf scanned the brothers, sizing up their reactions.

Abjörn leaned back in his chair, his brow furrowing deep. He wasn't just interested in helping to protect the settlement, Beecham Castle was now his home, and his wife laid her head here.

"What is your reason for being here? What is your group really after?" Abjörn asked.

Arne and Ulf shared another look before casting their eyes to the floor.

"What orders has the King given?" Sören groaned.

"Answer us!" Ryker's voice boomed.

"We cannot say. It is not our place. If the King's orders are to be discussed, you will have to speak to our commander Lief," Ulf answered.

Sören, Abjörn, and Ryker shared a perplexed look. What was going on in their homelands that now affected the shores they called home?

"Then we will speak with Lief upon his return," Abjörn concluded.

The room fell silent; everyone glanced around for a sign other than what sat across their faces. Frustration.

THE END

BODIL

SWORN TO PROTECT

PROLOGUE

ULF AND ARNE were keen on having a subject change. They knew the brothers were not happy being kept in the dark about the King's orders, but there was nothing Ulf nor Arne could say. It was not their place. If they discussed the King's orders without Lief, they would surely be in trouble with their commander. Knowing that the Highlanders and the English were working together against the Vikings, they had a new problem to worry about. The rest of the group travelled to the Point and were blissfully unaware.

"We need to warn Lief and the others. They have no idea what forces they are up against, and they are outnumbered," informed Ulf. "How can we warn them? Is there a quicker way to the Point from here?" He surveyed the surroundings, the rocky terrain beyond the forest and grasslands where Beecham Castle was situated. The ocean was nearby.

"From there, you will need one hell of a sailor and a strong ship. It's a rocky coast, but the trip can be made with the right crew. You won't make it to them on time if you travel by land," Sören answered; Ryker and Abjörn nodded their agreement.

"The sooner we leave, the better. Ulf and I shall leave right away. Sören, can we count on your support with your best ship and crew?" Arne enquired.

"You can," Sören agreed.

"Then it is settled. Ulf and Arne shall travel back to the settlement to gather the ship and leave with the tide. If the seas are with you, then you should make it to the Point in time to meet your comrades." Abjörn declared.

Everyone prepared to leave when Coline stepped forward. She was not happy with the plan. Arne had a positive influence on her. Sima noticed a change in her sister, from the wilted wallflower to a strong thorny rose, a woman who knew her mind and was no longer scared to speak it.

"I am not leaving Arne. Instead, I shall travel with you," she declared.

"Absolutely not," Arne boomed.

"I can help," Coline protested.

Ulf looked around the room, amused by how everyone enjoyed the couple arguing. Although, he had to admit he admired how Coline stood her ground.

"How exactly?" Sima interjected. It was an intelligent move; she wanted Arne to think that she was on her side, but she was actually giving her sister a chance to fight her case.

"MacTavish, the Scottish Laird who lives not far from the Point. He was an ally of our father. I can pretend to be on the run from the Vikings and scout for information." Coline explained.

The room fell silent as everyone mulled over her plan. It would be helpful to have someone behind enemy lines.

"Absolutely not!" Sima yelled, much to Arne's relief. "Coline, while I admire this newfound confidence in you, that is absolutely out of the question. It's far too dangerous. If MacTavish discovers you are there under false pretences, you will be his prisoner. Heaven knows what he will do to you."

Coline looked to Arne, who stood nodding, arms folded triumphantly. If Coline wouldn't listen to him, she would surely listen to Sima.

The brothers and their brides all stood together, sharing in the meeting. The brothers valued their wives' opinions as much as any of their soldiers. Astrid stood shoulder to shoulder with Ryker; she had proven herself in battle and was skilled with strategy.

Stepping forward, Astrid offered her solution before the arguing continued, and the ship missed the tide.

"I may have a solution that will please both parties." Astrid waited for everyone to stop and listen before continuing her plan. "Bodil is one of the best warriors I have ever had the honour of fighting beside. If dressed in the right way, she could easily play the part of a Lady's maid. She would act as Coline's bodyguard."

Ryker patted Astrid on the shoulder in admiration before pulling her back to him and burying his face in her neck. Much to her protests at the display of affection in the company of his brothers. But by the smile on her face, it was evident that she was still very much in love.

"It is a good plan. However, my concern is this. Bodil is not long widowed; she still grieves. Is her mind going to be on the task at hand? And will she agree while still in mourning?" Sören put forth.

"If her mind is not on the task, I stand by Sima. It is too dangerous for Coline," Arne stood firm.

"There are many lives at stake, Arne. It is not just about Coline. Our brothers in arms are in danger on their journey. The settlement could be attacked, and what of the King? What of Denmark? This Bodil woman is a Viking. Mourning or not, she is a warrior. She has a duty to perform," Ulf boomed, silencing the room.

His outburst may have been harsh, but he took his mission with the utmost seriousness. He cared deeply for his comrades and fellow Vikings. War was on the horizon, and they needed to prepare.

CHAPTER 1

BODIL DIDN'T NEED MUCH CONVINCING to accompany Coline, Arne, and Ulf on the expedition to the Point. She was more than happy for the change of scenery and to escape the settlement for a while. She had a secret, a deception that she had hidden for far too long. A chance to be around others who did not know her well was a welcome change.

Standing on the ship's deck, she felt the sway of the waves under her feet. With the sea breeze on her face and the beautiful view of the hills, she thought over her current situation.

She was a new widow. A woman in mourning, or so from the outside, it may have seemed. In reality, she had despised her late husband Gorm. He had won her over with lies, sweet words, and promises of a glorious future. But, once married, his true nature crept out from the darkness of his heart. He had been a cruel man, not just with his fists, but with his words. Bodil was a warrior, but under Gorm's shadow, she crumbled. She hid her shame under the pretence of being the lost widow, but in truth, she was glad he was dead. She was free.

She kept the truth about her relationship hidden behind closed doors, with fake smiles and a bowed head. Yet since Gorm's death, everyone had treated her so kindly and carefully. She hated lying to those she called friends, and worse, to family. But at sea, she wasn't just free from Gorm's memory, she was free from the lies, and free to finally breathe and be herself again.

The ship sailed off down the coast, leaving the settlement behind. Out of view of those she hid herself from, she closed her eyes and smiled as the sea's salt spray tickled her skin. The sea was freedom; it was change. Bodil allowed herself a moment to laugh at how her life had changed in such a short time. Arne and Coline had crept below deck while the rest of the crew busied themselves sailing the ship through the rocky waters. Bodil had imagined she was alone, but the creaking of wood underfoot alerted her that she was not.

Straightening, she glanced over her shoulder to see one of the newcomers who went by the name of Ulf. He was shorter than his comrades but still held a fair height. He was of a stocky build with broad shoulders and thick thighs like tree trunks. A small scar ran across his left cheek, hidden by the thick black beard that grew long down to his chest. If he didn't stare at her with a look of such disapproval, she would think of him as attractive. But the harshness of his gaze vexed her.

"Is there a problem?" Bodil asked defensively.

Ulf's face softened, and he gently shook his head, "I must be mistaken; I was informed you were recently widowed."

"Your point?"

"You do not appear to be in mourning. Laughing and smiling are not usually the traits of a widow," Ulf replied.

"Whether I laugh, smile, cry, or punch holes in the ship, it is none of your business how I mourn," Bodil snapped back. She turned to leave, but Ulf was not finished.

He grabbed her arm, stopping her, pulling her closer so she could hear his words clearly.

"When you are tasked with protecting the woman of my dearest friend, it *is* my business. You do not appear to be taking the task seriously."

"You question how I grieve, and now you question my morals? I assure you. I take my mission very seriously," Bodil snapped, pulling her arm free.

"I will admit I have never been truly in love. I have never married and never felt the sting of a love lost. But to laugh so soon after such a thing? I have seen the fall of the bravest of men. And frankly, it must make you foolhardy or a very cold-hearted woman indeed to be so joyful during this time." Ulf spoke.

For a second, Bodil stood flabbergasted. She had not expected a stranger to judge her so harshly. He knew not of her story, but his words brought up a memory that she was trying to escape from. Ulf eyed her up and down, his eyes lingering on her face.

"You seem to be a warm enough woman. There is a softness to your eyes that speaks of someone who cares deeply. I have seen that look before. I doubt you are as cold-hearted as that, so you must be a fool."

Bodil felt her blood boil. She had had her fill with men thinking they could judge, degrade, and mock her. She was free of Grom and would no longer take harsh words from anyone. She cared not for banter, be it ill meant or in jest. And she considerably disliked being toyed with, considerably. Mimicking his actions, she eyed him head to toe, glaring intensely into his dark blue eyes.

"If you like, I can introduce you to the end of my sword, and you can see just how cold-hearted I can be. I am not a fool, certainly not enough to waste my time with idiotic Vikings like you who have nothing better to do than question why a woman laughs." She snarled through clenched teeth before leaving him on the deck alone.

Furious with the stranger named Ulf, Bodil decided to seek out the company of Coline. She was sure Arne would not mind her interrupting as she needed to learn what she could about her for the mission at hand. Plus, she found that she grew quite fond of the girl who belonged to Arne. She was learning a lot from Coline. And after her encounter with Ulf, Bodil thought it would be nice to have an ally on the trip.

CHAPTER 2

"APOLOGIES FOR INTERRUPTING. I was hoping to check in with Coline," Bodil said as she knocked on the door to the cabin that Arne and Coline resided inside.

"Your timing couldn't be better," Arne smiled.

Bodil noticed Coline laying in the cot with a damp cloth on her forehead, and an arm dropped over her eyes. A bucket sat on the floor next to her. Coline looked positively green. She had not gained her sea legs; the sea wasn't treating her well.

"I'm afraid I am not coping well," Coline croaked, lurching forward to empty her stomach in the bucket. "I have not had the pleasure of being abroad on a ship such as this before. It may take a while for me to adjust," she tried to smile as Arne passed her another cup of water from the barrel in the corner.

"I shall care for her," Bodil said, kneeling beside her bed.

Arne kissed Coline gently and allowed the women some time alone. The smell of sick lay thick in the air; it wasn't aiding Coline's current state.

"Perhaps some fresh air will ease your stomach. The smell in here is quite thick." Bodil winced, scrunching her nose, and moving the bucket further away.

"If you think it may help," Coline agreed.

"Learning to walk on the ship, working with the sea's motion, should also help. Come, I will assist you," Bodil took Coline's arm and helped her to her feet.

Growing up in court with her feet planted firmly on land, Coline was miserable at sea. Bodil remembered her first time abroad a ship, the first time she sailed into treacherous waters. How the bobbing and swaying of the open ocean had her stomach turning and her head spinning. Thankfully, she had sailed a lot since then and knew how to handle the sea.

Walking up onto the deck, Bodil held tight to Coline, talking her through how to feel the ship's sway and predict a rise in the waves. After a few more steps, Coline appeared to be making progress, that is until Bodil saw the tell-tale flash in her eyes. Guiding her to the ship's side, Coline heaved forward, emptying the remainder of her breakfast into the waters below.

"How embarrassing. I am with a mighty Viking, yet I cannot keep my bearings when at sea," Coline groaned.

"Do not worry, Coline. Even us Vikings have to gain our sea legs at one time or another," Bodil smiled reassuringly.

Night approached over the horizon as the hour was late. Bodil agreed to let Coline catch a little more air before laying her head down for the night. The air was warm, a little too warm for Bodil's liking, while the sea was too cold. It never made for a good combination while sailing rocky shores. A fog began to form; Bodil knew this would make an already risky journey that bit trickier.

Coline watched Bodil closely; it was evident that she was concerned.

"You appear worried. What are you afraid of?"

Bodil took a deep breath, trying to figure out how to her answer. She didn't want to frighten the poor girl who had a reputation for scaring easily, especially when she was already struggling with the trip. Opening her mouth to answer, her words fell silent as the ship boomed, making contact with rocks below. The boat shook, causing Bodil and Coline to stagger, struggling to stand.

Stumbling, Arne and Ulf came running to their aid. Bodil just managed to grab Coline's hand as the ship pitched sideways, flinging the woman overboard. Hanging from Bodil's hand, Coline screamed and clawed at the side of the vessel, trying to pull herself up. Another boom sounded, followed by a loud creaking of strained wood as the ship rocked again, sending both Boil and Coline overboard.

Arne and Ulf arrived just in time to dive down, following the women tumbling into the icy waters below.

"Coline?" yelled Bodil swimming through the cold, trying to avoid the rocks barely visible through the fog and night air.

The wind was picking up; the tide was not being kind, smashing against Bodil. The cold bit at her skin, making her bones ache. Treading water, Bodil struggled as waves crashed against the ship, sending her under more than once.

"Coline!?" she yelled again.

Looking up at the ship that still rocked to one side, Bodil calculated the fall, figuring out where Coline might have landed. She hadn't heard her cry out; Coline never responded to her calls. Bodil panicked, swimming out to the section of rocks that held the bow of the ship captive, hoping and praying to the gods that Coline hadn't struck her head and been taken under by the current.

Her pursuit was dropped as Ulf grabbed her, dragging her towards the inlet where the water shallowed.

"Head to shore," he bellowed over the crashing waves.

"I must find Coline," Bodil protested, attempting to free herself from Ulf's mighty hand.

"Arne has her, now get to shore!" he boomed.

Following swiftly behind, Bodil followed Ulf to shore. She was still uneasy and occasionally glanced back to make sure Coline was, in fact, no longer in the water.

CHAPTER 3

ON SHORE, Bodil assessed the scene. Arne, Ulf, and she thankfully hadn't sustained any injuries. And thankfully, the ship wasn't too severely damaged. But it would take time to free the ship from the rocks, delaying their efforts to reach the Point in time to warn Lief and the others. It was the last thing they needed at such a crucial time. From what she could tell, it had only been the four of them tossed overboard. From the crew on the ship calling for them, they had noticed they were missing.

Bodil sat. She was furious with herself; how had she managed to let Coline fall? How was she not able to keep the two of them aboard the ship? She was a skilled sailor and a strong, mighty warrior. She had faced worst waters than this.

"Is everyone alright?" Arne queried.

"Yes," Ulf groaned in response.

"I'm not fine. I should have been steadier. It's my job to keep Coline safe, and I failed at the first hurdle," Bodil complained, louder than she had expected as the group heard.

"It was not your fault. We were making too much haste. The crew misjudged our position in the fog. We should have been further away from shore. It was an amateur mistake," Ulf argued.

"Freeing the ship will delay us even further," Arne stomped.

"I thought Sören had given us his best crew. They are supposed to know these waters," Ulf argued.

Bodil ignored the men bickering and travelled up the beach to Coline, who shivered in the cold and looked a little shaken up. Amid their bellyaching, neither of them had thought to check on her, which vexed Bodil even more.

"Will you two shut up? For the love of the gods, you sound like young school girls. Stop being so stupid and blaming others; it was no one's fault. We knew these waters were a danger. Men and their inflated egos, neither of you cared to check on Coline," Bodil snapped in frustration.

Arne rushed to Coline's side, apologizing profusely. Coline insisted that she was fine despite the large slice down her calf. It wasn't broken from what Bodil could see, but it would be difficult to walk on while it healed.

"There is a small village up the coast. We could get horses and supplies and continue our journey. We are delayed now anyway; at least this way, we can keep going," Coline winced as Arne tended to her wound.

"We could see about getting the ship repaired and follow on," Bodil suggested.

A few crew members descended from the ship aboard a smaller vessel to aid their recovery. Arne refused to let anyone else tend to Coline, blaming himself for not getting to her sooner.

"You, boy!" Ulf asked, pointing to a crew member barely old enough to hold a sword. "Do you know these lands well?"

The boy nodded confidently, "I do."

"How far to the Highlander's castle?"

The boy looked around, surveying the surroundings as best he could through the thickening fog.

"Half a day's ride if you make haste."

"I can still make the journey," Coline insisted even as she struggled to hide her pain.

Trying to stand, her leg buckled, and she fell into Arne's waiting arms.

"Not a chance. You are hurt; you need to heal. If you make the journey, you risk infection. We do not have the herbs to treat such wounds. I will take you back to the ship. Ulf and Bodil can travel to the village and gather what we need to repair the ship, and we carry on as planned," Arne insisted.

"We can't afford to argue. We don't have time to waste. There is no other way to find the information we need," Coline pleaded, but Arne was adamant that she was in no fit state to continue.

"We will have to find another way. It was a risky plan at best. Now, look what has happened. How would you explain to the Laird that you managed to get on horseback when you can't even stand?" Arne scolded.

Coline opened her mouth to argue, but Arne had his own mission he was fighting. Protecting her.

"No, Coline. If something were to go wrong if he figured out your plan, how would you escape?"

Coline fell silent, she didn't want to admit he was right, but he fought a good case. Their plan was as dead in the water, as was the remains of their ship. A thought sparked in Bodil's mind. One she knew would work. The plan Coline had come up with was too good to risk abandoning. They needed that information from the Laird, and she would get it one way or the other.

"Coline, this MacTavish, has he lain eyes on you before? Would he know your hair is red? Is there any way he can identify you?"

"No, he met my sister Sima and my father, but we were never formally introduced. Why do you ask?"

Ulf and Arne hung on Bodil's every word. Her heart picked up pace as a new hope grew within her. She could keep her promise of protecting Coline by leaving her behind with Arne and travelling in her place, posing as the young Lady.

"I shall go in your place. I know enough of the language to pass as a Highlander. It is a good plan, no? This way, Coline can stay with Arne and the ship and follow on when it is repaired, and we can still go ahead with our plan."

Ulf shook his head, his face growing grim and firm. She might say he cared if Bodil didn't know any better, but she dared not wonder after their earlier disagreement.

"It's far too risky for a woman alone. Even for a warrior such as yourself," Ulf argued.

"Then she won't go alone. Someone should go and keep watch from the cover of the hills. Then, if she feels she is in danger, she could raise the alarm. I'm sure Bodil can manage herself until help arrives," Arne suggested.

Running a frustrated hand over his face and rubbing his temples, Ulf groaned out. His mind raced with possibilities for failure.

"You need to stay with Coline. Someone needs to take the ship the rest of the way to the Point.... I will watch over Bodil," Ulf declared.

Bodil was not happy with his declaration. She knew that he thought little of her as it was and didn't want or need his supervision.

"I have no need for a nursemaid. I can take care of myself. I have taken down Celts, Highlanders, and English alike. I can handle a Laird."

Ulf and Bodil began to argue amongst themselves. He thought her foolish for wanting to risk going alone. And she plainly didn't like him. It was bad enough being forced to work with a man who clearly thought so little of her without even knowing her or offering the chance to get to know her. She was free from the constraints of her husband's scorn. She didn't fancy being under another man's boot so soon.

"Enough!" Arne yelled, his voice travelling far on the wind. "Either Ulf goes with you, or no one goes. This is no time for arguing. We have people relying on us. While we argue between ourselves, our enemy makes advances against us."

Ulf and Bodil glared at each other. Then, silently agreed to make the trip together because Arne was right, even if they didn't want to admit it. They needed each other to get the job done.

CHAPTER 4

ULF ORDERED the crew members to head to the village to fetch horses while Coline continued to coach Bodil on the ways of castle life back on the ship. The correct way to greet a Laird, when and who to call M'Lord or M'Lady. Bodil was a quick study, but Coline didn't have time to teach her everything she needed to know, just the basics to get by.

"If he asks about the village you escaped from, what do you say?" Coline asked.

"Please, M'Lord, I would rather not discuss it. It has been an ordeal I would much rather forget," Bodil answered, bowing her head, and playing the part of a damsel in distress perfectly.

Ulf grunted and rolled his eyes.

"Have something to say, Oaf…. sorry, I mean Ulf?" Bodil teased, making Coline hide her laugh behind her sleeve. She was so happy to be on dry land again.

"I think this plan is foolish. You barely know the language and you are not truly versed in the ways of the court. You will be made before the sun sets."

"You speak like you wish the plan to fail," Bodil snipped.

"Don't be so foolish. I wish the plan to succeed as much as the next person. However, I cannot see how you are supposed to pass as a Lady of the King's court." Ulf groaned.

Coline had set aside one of her dresses for Bodil. She rolled her eyes and slipped behind the stack of barrels to change from her travelling clothes into that of a Lady. Bodil was a touch bigger than Coline. Her hips were wider, her buttocks higher, and her breasts were sizably different. The dress fit, but it highlighted everything twice as much as it would if worn by Coline. Stepping from behind the barrels, now fully dressed for her new role, Bodil tucked a small knife into the top of her boot, hidden by the floor-length skirt.

"Now she looks the part of a Lady of the court," Coline breathed.

Arne whistled, and Ulf finally shot a look in her direction. His jaw fell open, and his eyes bulged. She was a vision.

"My, I believe you have rendered him speechless. But take note, it doesn't happen often." Arne teased.

Bodil felt her cheeks blush under Ulf's longing stare. Then, breaking his gaze, he coughed and headed for the door.

"We should make haste," Ulf grunted, closing the door behind him.

Ulf, Arne, and Bodil sailed from the ship back to shore to the waiting horses. No one said anything; Bodil fiddled with the bodice, uncomfortable in the restricting fabric. Arne grinned to himself, watching his friend try not to stare at the beauty who sat across from him.

Ulf offered Bodil a hand in mounting her horse, but she knocked his hand aside and jumped astride without needing his help. Turning her horse away from him, she listened to the directions the crew boy gave her to the castle.

"Good luck, brother," Arne chuckled, setting sail back to the ship.

Riding ahead, Ulf fought with his mind. He couldn't stop his eyes from roaming Bodil's curves and admiring how the bodice pushed her breasts high, framing them perfectly. Grunting to himself, finally, he decided to speak.

"I still think this is a foolish endeavour."

"Not this again," Bodil sighed.

"I don't see why we can't simply travel to the village and ask questions. Surely someone will know something."

Bodil laughed hard at his statement "And you say I know nothing of the court."

"What is that supposed to mean?"

"The villagers rarely know anything of the Lord's affairs. They are reminded early on of their place. Taught to keep their noses out of business above their station. If we start asking questions, word will make it to the Laird before we or the others reach the Point," Boil mocked.

"I thought the villagers are warned to stay out of the ranking affairs," Ulf tried to make jest of her statement.

"That is true, but do not be fooled. The best spies are the ones who are ruled by fear. Do you wish something to befall me?"

"What?" Ulf gasped.

"You heard me. I might add that you seem so set on ruining our plan, which is a good plan. I will likely be caught up in it if word makes it to the Lord of a plot afoot. If I didn't know any better, I would say you wish ill on this cold heart of mine," Bodil sneered, using his words against him.

Ulf pulled his horse closer to hers and grabbed for her reigns, pulling both steeds to a stop. Bodil turned to him in surprise, even more so when he leaned forward and laid his lips on hers. She didn't pull back as he continued his task, kissing her breathless before abruptly pulling away and marching his horse onwards.

Bodil sat atop her horse, watching Ulf ride on. For the first time in the longest, she found that she was speechless. *What on earth just happened?*

CHAPTER 5

TRUE TO THE word of the crew boy, half a day after leaving the ship, the castle came into view. It was not as vast as Beacham Castle but still impressive. The castle had stone walls surrounding it and guards were posted every few feet armed with shields and spears.

"I shall watch from the cover of the hills. I will keep a close eye. If danger presents itself, set a fire. When I see the smoke, I shall come," Ulf instructed.

"I can handle myself," Bodil insisted, preparing to finish her ride to the castle. Instead, Ulf took her arm and stared at her, his gaze freezing her, making her want to listen.

"I do not doubt your ability; you come highly recommended. My statement still stands. Set a fire; I shall be by your side," Ulf breathed.

His words carried more weight with Bodil than she expected. Nodding her agreement, Ulf whispered for her to be safe before dismounting and sneaking off into the trees. Bodil sat watching until she could no longer see him before she rode in a daze towards Laird MacTavish's castle.

The guards didn't question a Lady, allowing her to pass. When she dismounted, her horse was swiftly taken to the stables while two guards led her through the darkened halls to MacTavish, who was still sitting down to eat.

"Laird MacTavish, I present Lady Coline Beecham, second

daughter to Lord Beacham," announced the guards leaving Bodil standing under MacTavish's watchful eye.

MacTavish was old and looked stronger than a man of his age. Bodil stooped into a curtsy, her eyes not leaving MacTavish as he leered over her.

"What brings you to my castle, Lady Coline?" MacTavish croaked, sucking his fingers as food slid down his hands.

The sight turned Bodil's stomach, but she kept her act up.

"I come seeking aid. I believe you were a friend to my father. Our castle was set upon by Vikings. I was held in a village they raided. I managed to escape. I stole a horse and rode for days. Please, M'lord, you are the only one who can help me. I beg for shelter," Bodil pleaded, making her eyes big and bowing her head.

"Impressive for a young woman to escape Vikings unscathed," MacTavish sneered, his eyes on her breasts.

"I feared for my life M'lord. My family are all still prisoners; I could not save them. I was hoping I may beg your assistance."

"And how am I to do that?"

"I am not versed in war or combat, M'lord," Bodil bowed her head.

"How did you manage to escape?"

"It is all such a blur. I was sent to fetch water and saw the gates had been left ajar. I ran to the stables and rode off as fast as I could," Bodil feigning a tear, making her voice croak, and hiding her dry eyes in her hands.

She knew MacTavish grew suspicious and hoped he would give up his line of questioning before she ran out of answers.

"You must be tired, my girl. My guards will show you to a bed-chamber where you may wish to get some rest. I shall come to see you on the morrow to discuss matters further."

Two guards closed in on Bodil. Suddenly, she felt she was no longer a guest in this castle but a prisoner in a very nice cage.

"Thank you, M'lord, your hospitality is greatly appreciated," Bodil smiled sweetly, batting her eyelashes.

MacTavish continued leering, but waved her away, dismissing her and the guards.

The castle was deceptive from the outside. It looked so small, but as the guards walked Bodil through, she felt the halls went on and on. Finally, they opened the door to what looked like a servant's quarters in the back of the castle. The shutters on the window were locked by a thick padlock, and the room stank of musk and dampness. The cot was barely standing, and the fireplace looked unusable. Shoving her inside, the guards slammed the heavy door, and Bodil heard the clink of a key as their footsteps vanished back down the halls.

Trapped in her room, Bodil paced the small space, kicking the leg of the cot each time she passed. MacTavish said he would be visiting her in the morning; she needed the night to figure out exactly how she could convince him she was, in fact, Coline. If he remembered Lord Beecham, he might remember how young his youngest daughter was. While Bodil was no old maid, she was a handful of years older than Coline and looked as such.

Laying on the cot, trying to get comfortable as night fell, Bodil was surprised when she heard the clink of the key and saw Ulf stride in.

"How are you here? Why are you here? I did not signal you to come," Bodil whispered angrily, even though she was secretly happy about his arrival.

"I didn't trust those guards. I thought it better to keep a close eye on you from inside," Ulf whispered, closing the door behind him.

"Well, in truth, you couldn't have come at a better time. I feel you are right. He does not believe me to be Coline. This plan was a mistake."

Ulf said nothing, surprised by her admission. They had clashed a lot in their brief time knowing one another. And from what Ulf had seen of her, he knew she wouldn't admit being wrong lightly.

"Perhaps….no…. maybe," Bodil wondered aloud, pacing the small room, made even smaller by Ulf's large frame.

"Speak, woman," Ulf grinned.

"The old goat couldn't keep his eyes off me. He barely looked at my face…. the same way you are looking now," Bodil snapped, whacking a hand across Ulf's shoulder, causing him to chuckle lightly. "Perhaps I could seduce him. Maybe that would gain his trust enough to loosen his tongue."

Ulf raised one of his thick eyebrows, folding his arms across his chest and leaning against the door. His eyes travelled the length of her once again.

"You seem so easy with your body for someone who has recently been widowed."

Bodil grew tired of his accusations. She grew tired of having her actions questioned, especially since she was in this position to help him and his friends.

"I believe it was you who kissed me, not the other way around," she retorted.

When Ulf's self-pleased expression sat unchanged, Bodil felt that she needed to explain herself further, despite her annoyance in having to do so.

"Besides, I do not intend to do THAT. Have you seen MacTavish? He is disgusting. He just needs to *think* I intend to lay with him."

Ulf's grin widened, he seemed amused by her efforts. Either that or he didn't believe she had it in her to do it.

"He may be old, but he is no fool. He shall see right through you."

Bodil sensed the challenge in his tone. She was a warrior in more ways than one, and she knew how to use her womanhood to her advantage. From Ulf's stance and the amused look in his eyes, Bodil formed a new plan. If her words did not convince Ulf that she was capable of seducing the Laird, then her actions would.

"Oh, Ulf, you are right; I was foolish to think I could do this alone," she sighed, allowing her shoulders to sag and her head to fall in mock defeat.

"I am?" Ulf asked in surprise.

"Yes, I do not know what I would do if you had not come when you did. Look at me; I am unarmed in this hideous dress that I cannot move or breathe in, helpless to MacTavish and his men," she said, pulling uncomfortably at the seams of her dress.

Ulf's eyes fell to the bodice, which Bodil tugged, trying to free herself.

"I am a warrior, not a Lady. I look as ridiculous as I feel. I am simply trying to prove I still have a purpose in this world."

"I think you have a purpose....and you look anything but ridiculous," Ulf gulped. Bodil knew that she had been successful in her scheme to show him her talents of seduction.

Bodil batted her eyes and blushed, edging closer to him, stroking his arm while passing him a coy smile.

"Your words are too kind. But I will admit, I feel safer knowing you are here to protect me.... you and these big strong arms," she teased, stroking his arm, and allowing her hands to roam up to his shoulders and down his chest. She sucked in a gasp. She looked at him with lust-filled eyes, her fingers started clawing at the wall of muscle beneath them.

"Can I tell you something?" she asked, pressing her breasts against him, trying to steady her breath.

"Anything," Ulf gulped.

Bodil leaned close to his ear and sighed gently, her hands slipping under his shirt to feel the smooth skin of his stomach.

"I haven't been able to stop thinking about that kiss. No man has ever kissed me in such a way.... with such unbridled passion, it had me wondering.... but no, I shouldn't," she whispered, pulling herself away.

It was enough to make Ulf want to hear more, grabbing her shoulders and holding her in place.

"Wondering what Bodil?" he asked groggily.

She smiled and bent to his ear, nipping lightly in his ear lobe as her hands slid lower.

"It had me wondering what other passion you were capable of...."

Before finishing her sentence, Ulf had scooped her in his arms and carried her to the bed, pinning her beneath him.

His hands made quick work of untying the bodice, finally freeing her breasts. Ulf sucked on her nipples while one hand pinned her hands clasped above her head and the other hurried up her skirt.

Bodil moaned out at his touch and moved her legs to open wide, allowing Ulf's hands to trace her inner thigh. She intertwined her fingers with his as best she could, letting him know she wanted it too.... much to her surprise.

Ulf ran kisses up her chest and neck, finally bringing his lips back down on hers where her mouth welcomed him. She moaned against his lips as his fingers teased the dampness between her thighs.

She pulled her hands free and reached down to his waistline, urging him to free himself. Ulf felt her advancements and readied himself to oblige. Pushing his trousers down, Bodil gasped at the sight. Ulf stood to attention, his cock erect, begging for her touch. He wasn't overly long, but his girth was impressive, and Bodil felt herself twitch in response. Anticipation built in the pit of her stomach.

Rolling her skirts up in a hurry, mentally cursing the layers of fabric, she pulled Ulf down on top of her, ready to welcome him when their escapades were interrupted by a knock on the door.

"Lady Coline," croaked MacTavish, "are you still awake?"

CHAPTER 6

"IT'S MACTAVISH!" Bodil whispered as she hurried to redress.

The room was small, and there was not much furniture or places to hide, and with the windows being locked, there was no way for Ulf to escape.

Ulf barely made it under the cot before the old Laird burst through the door, surprising Bodil with how agile the old man was.

"My dear, I have not been able to stop thinking of you. I could not wait till the morrow," he cooed, rushing to her, and grabbing at her hips.

"How kind of you to worry about me," she cooed.

"You must be so frightened after your ordeal. Look at you. You are still trembling," the Laird ran a hand through her hair and stroked her cheek.

She was indeed trembling, but not for the reasons he thought.

"Let me look at you. Are you sure those brute Vikings did not hurt you?" he asked. His hands roamed over her hungrily. "A pretty thing like you. So young and supple."

Bodil fought to not roll her eyes, grabbing his hands and moving them away from places his hands had no business being. She could feel the blade in her boot. Taking comfort, she knew it was one swift move away from finding a home between MacTavish's ribs.

"My Lord, while I would be happy to show my gratitude for your assistance and shelter, I can't help but worry if I am truly safe here. What if I had been followed?"

"If you were followed, my dear, we would know about it by now."

MacTavish pulled at Bodil's dress harder, trying to stop her from pulling away. She glanced over his shoulder to see Ulf's eyes peering from under the bed. She shook her head, sensing him growing angry and wanting to intervene.

"My Lord, while I would like to thank you, I cannot concentrate. I worry. I am concerned…." Bodil spoke frantically, trying to control the Laird's wandering hands.

She was now happy she had taken Coline's place. Bodil was strong enough to hold off the Laird's advances; she feared Coline would not have been so lucky.

"My Lord, please," Bodil snapped, pushing hard on his shoulders, finally breaking free. Then, taking a breath, she softened her resolve on seeing the frustration in his eyes.

"If we can solve the issue of my safety, we can continue our time together in a much more relaxed setting. Don't you agree?"

"There is no issue with your safety," MacTavish lunged at Bodil, pulling her once again into his embrace, trying to kiss her.

"What if the Vikings show up? Are your castle and guards strong enough to hold off an attack?"

Frustrated, MacTavish groaned loudly in one long breath. Then, slowing, his mauling stopped, and he gave them exactly what they wanted.

"There are plenty of troops guarding my castle. Not just my men, but a group is arriving from England any day now."

"From England?"

"Yes! Under the command of Lord William Thomas. Now stop worrying and thank me properly for allowing you to take sanctuary in my castle."

MacTavish buried his face in the crook of Bodil's neck, his hands roaming around to cup her buttocks. Bodil locked eyes with Ulf and mouthed, "do you know of a Lord William Thomas?"

Ulf shook his head, mystified.

"I do not know of this Lord William Thomas. Do you trust him?" Bodil enquired.

"I'm tired of all these questions!" Laird MacTavish roared, spinning Bodil around and flinging her on the bed.

Bodil cried out as her head bounced off the wall. MacTavish didn't get very far before Ulf roared out from under the bed charging at the Laird, slamming him into the opposite wall.

MacTavish fell silent, his face a wash of shock and horror. The old man may have been agile and strong enough to maul Bodil, but he didn't stand a chance against Ulf. His eyes wide with fear. He began to tremble, never had the Laird expected to be set upon in the confines of his own castle.

Ulf pulled a knife from his waist and raised it to the Laird's throat, "you Lords all think you are better than everyone else. What gives you the right to maltreat a young Lady like that? Your castle and lands do not give you the right to treat another person like your plaything, especially a defenceless young woman who came to you for help." Ulf stopped, realising his outburst.

He hadn't meant to make his outburst about Bodil, but he detested how the Laird had pawed at her. The way he threw her onto the bed and when she cried out had been the final straw.

"I say we kill him. He is no use to us now," Ulf grunted, pushing the blade harder on the old man's throat.

Bodil jumped up and grabbed Ulf's arm stopping him from making a huge mistake. The guards would notice if the Laird was missing, and the blame would instantly fall on her since she was the only outsider in the castle.

"I didn't know you cared so much," she teased; it worked, as she felt his shoulders loosen.

"If we kill him, we will bring the entire household down on our heads. How would I explain a dead Laird in my bed-chamber on the same night I call asking for shelter? Let's be reasonable. He may still prove of use. Here..." She tore a strip of fabric from the blanket, "let's bind and gag him. Lock him in the wardrobe until we need him again."

Ulf didn't move, and MacTavish stayed silent. A slight tug of his arm and Ulf caved, seeing sense in Bodil's plan.

CHAPTER 7

With MacTavish safely bound and locked in his wardrobe, Ulf and Bodil made their escape, closing the door behind them. Ulf took tight hold of Bodil's hand, guiding her through the darkened halls the way he had entered through the servant's quarters and past the kitchens.

The guards hadn't noticed MacTavish was missing. So they went about their business as usual as night fell. Ulf noticed how their work ethic lacked. Some slept at their posts while others stood chatting. None of them had seen Bodil and Ulf running towards the stables.

Making quick work of saddling horses, the conversation turned to what their plan was now.

"What is the plan?" Bodil whispered.

"I don't know. We need to warn the others, but it would be good to know how big a force we are up against....no it's too risky. We are outnumbered, and you don't have your sword. So, we carry on to the Point. By the time we make it there, the others will have caught up with the ship." Ulf answered.

"We know the Lord's name. Wouldn't it be better to spy on the approaching forces and learn his face?"

"You are crazy. No, we go to the Point; reinforcements will be waiting for us there," Ulf argued.

"What is the point in warning them if we do not know what force we are up against? This Lord Thomas may have no real army at all for all we know. There is no use in creating undue panic."

"That was never the plan. We got what we came for."

"Why are you so stubborn? The mission is still the same; we came to find information, and now we have a new lead to follow up on. The plan is unchanged. Arne and the ship will warn the others of the English and Highlander alliance," Bodil retorted.

Ulf thought over her words. She was right. The plan had been to warn Lief, which is what Arne was doing. Bodil had taken on Coline's identity for a fact-finding mission, but they still had information they needed to find. As he looked at her, as she waited for his response, his mind changed again. It was a good plan, Bodil was right, but she still looked like a Lady of the King's court and had no armour or weapons. The thought that she might be hurt, or captured, left bile rising up his throat.

"No..." he shook his head, unable to finish before Bodil shoved him hard in the chest, glaring at him with eyes full of thunder.

"Why? Why do you always do this? Why are my plans never good enough for you?" Bodil snapped.

"Look, it's nothing like that...."

"Then tell me why. Give me one good reason why we shouldn't hunt for the troops?"

The truth was he couldn't answer. How could he tell her the truth? That he didn't want to risk her being hurt? The way she had volunteered to take Coline's place, despite the danger it put her in, how she risked rocky waters to save a woman she barely knew and how she handled herself against MacTavish. Ulf wondered if he had misjudged her. She fought her case well, not just now but at every step of their journey. The longer he spent with her, the more his appreciation and affection for her grew.

"Well?" Bodil poked at his chest with a firm finger when he didn't answer.

"Fine, let us go with your plan," Ulf agreed.

CHAPTER 8

ACCORDING to the information they gathered from MacTavish before they gagged him and shoved him in the wardrobe, Lord William Thomas and his troops were heading to the castle from the south. It meant doubling back, going in the opposite direction of their comrades. But it was an opportunity they couldn't miss. They rode slowly, keeping to the tree line and off the main path. They needed the cover of the trees if they were to come upon the Lord and his troops.

At first, they didn't speak. What had happened between them in the castle still lay thick in the air. Neither wanting to address it. What would have happened if MacTavish hadn't interrupted? Bodil had only meant to prove a point, yet as Ulf attempted to ravage her, she realized how much she wanted it. The more she thought about it, the more uncomfortable riding became.

"I feel I should apologise," Ulf finally broke their silence.

"For what?"

"I have been too harsh on you. You put yourself at risk to protect Coline, and still, even when things seemed tense, your mind was on the mission. I see why Ryker's woman Astrid suggested you for the task," he admitted.

Bodil didn't know how to respond; she tried her best to hide her blushing cheeks at his compliment.

"Why were you so harsh? Do you have a problem with women?"

she asked, correcting herself at his pained look. "I mean, no offence, I'm just curious."

After a moment's thought, Ulf decided honesty was the best policy. Finally, opening up to her, to someone, about how he truly felt. A secret that had plagued his mind for too long.

"In truth? I do not feel I belong on this quest," he began. "My father is one of the King's most trusted advisors. So, he suggested that I go with Lief and the others."

"I'm sure your father believes in your abilities; otherwise, he wouldn't have suggested it."

"I know you are right; you are not the first to suggest so. I have many a battle under my belt. I have fought with Lief and Arne for as long as I can remember. That said, I wasn't Lief's first choice."

"I'm sure that's not true."

"No, it is. I was ok with that, but my father insisted. So now I feel I have to do something noble to prove myself. To prove to the King, Lief, and my father that the choice for me to join the mission was the right one."

"That's a lot to have on one's shoulders," Bodil said, feeling for Ulf and his struggle.

"Bodil, may I ask you something?"

"Of course,"

"Forgive me for being so bold, but how are you so.... calm after recently becoming a widow?" Ulf asked gently, sensing it may be a sensitive subject.

Bodil knew the subject of her husband would come back up eventually. That didn't mean she was happy about it. Yet she appreciated Ulf's candour about his father and his place on the mission. Honesty calls for honesty, after all. She took a moment to figure out where exactly to begin.

"Grom was.... a difficult man. Not at first. He had me fooled with sweet and kind words. Promises of the future, travel, and our own ship. As soon as he claimed me as his wife, all that changed. He was not the man I thought he was. Not the man I fell in love with," Bodil shared.

It was the first time she had spoken such words to anyone. Not even her closest friends and family knew of the horror that was her marriage. She had wanted to talk to someone, anyone, about Grom and his ways, but she felt deep shame. Was there something wrong with her for a man who claimed to have loved her to treat her so? She was a warrior. How had she allowed herself to be treated in such a way? Those were just a few of the many questions she had asked herself throughout her marriage.

"He was an angry man, especially when drunk. He would pick apart my swordsmanship, constantly telling me I was no warrior and not Viking or woman enough to be a shield or sword maiden. When I proved him wrong, he didn't like it and broke my arm. I informed Astrid that I had been tossed from my horse." She stopped checking Ulf out of the corner of her eye.

He listened intently, which she appreciated. He didn't say a word, waiting for her to continue; he knew she still had much to say.

"'Your place is in the home tending to me,' he had said. He didn't like me having any life of my own. My world had to stop and start with him. His words, his fists, I took them both," she choked. She didn't realize how much pain she still held on to.

"You are a warrior; why allow him to treat you so?" Ulf asked.

"Because I loved him. I was delusional. I accepted his apologies thinking things would get better. They never did," Bodil stopped.

Ulf opened his mouth to speak, feeling increasingly enraged when he heard of Grom's horrid ways. Even now, she never spoke of him with venom in her voice. Instead, she spoke simply of the hell she had endured. Ulf knew that she had every right to hate him, but her tone didn't depict a woman who hated anyone. Instead, her tone spoke of a woman who was now free.

"I fought back once. I had my fill, but all it did was make things worse. Gorm's ego couldn't allow him to be humiliated by a woman, not just any woman, the one he claimed as his.....He almost killed me that night.....You may think of me as cold-hearted for laughing and being so free, but you must understand, for the first time in years, I am just that. Free. I'm glad he is dead." She finished, straightening herself up, trying to hide the pain visible in her eyes.

"I am so sorry I misjudged you," Ulf admitted, guilt stabbing at him like a thorn in his side.

"You did not know."

"That is no excuse."

"I laugh, and I smile around you and your men because they do not know me or my story. They have not been the ones I have had to hide from. What kind of warrior allows herself to be a slave in her own home?"

"Enough! I will not hear you speak of yourself that way." Ulf snapped, much to Bodil's surprise.

"You are so much more than you know. You are loyal and caring, strong, and beautiful…. You should feel no shame for your choices; you loved him and stayed loyal to him despite his despicable actions against you. I, too, am glad he is dead…in fact, no, I wish he was still here so I could teach him a thing or two on how a man is supposed to treat his woman!" Ulf groaned, lost in his own thoughts.

Ulf had never been in love, never felt its warmth. But with Bodil, he found he was getting close. There were no other words to describe it, no other way to explain it. He cared for her well-being. Watching MacTavish paw at her, seeing her fall overboard, and now hearing the vile things her late husband had done. It was too much. Ulf felt his heartache a little more with each of her words. The thought of her having to walk through life with this huge secret, not being able to tell anyone, he couldn't imagine how that felt.

"Thank you, but I do not want your pity."

"You do not have my pity…. On the contrary, you have my admiration. How can you think you have anything less?" Ulf asked, once again leaving Bodil lost for words.

"Bodil, I…."

Bodil's face dropped, her eyes grew grave, and she grabbed the reigns of his horse, pulling it to a stop. She raised a finger to her lips and pointed to the hills ahead. A small army marched right towards them, moving quickly. Ulf guided their horses into the tree line out of sight.

CHAPTER 9

BODIL AND ULF dismounted and let the horses graze nearby. Then, they quickly climbed high into the treetops to stay out of sight. From a higher vantage point, they could see the group more clearly. On closer inspection, the group wasn't as large as Laird had made them out to be, maybe a dozen or more men followed by horses pulling wagons filled with supplies.

"These are the troops? We could take care of the threat here and now," Ulf whispered.

"Don't be a fool. These will not be the only troops; just the first."

"Exactly, slow them down and take their supplies before they can arm their forces," Ulf argued.

"It's too open, an attack on that many men in the light of day is foolish, and you know it," she snapped back.

Ulf looked at her reproachingly, hoping to entice the warrior in her. He longed to see her in battle after hearing the glowing stories from Astrid and Ryker.

"There are TWO of us. We could take them down without breaking a sweat." Ulf grinned, making his eyebrows dance.

Bodil had to admit it was tempting. But she still needed to arm herself and get out of the restricting dress into something better suited for battle.

"No, we wait until nightfall. Take them by surprise," she expected Ulf to argue, but he nodded his agreement and climbed down.

Under the cover of night, while most of the men slept, Bodil and Ulf circled the troop's camp like hungry lions sizing up their pray. Two men stood on guard by a tent much grander than the others, obviously housing Lord William Thomas. Signalling to Ulf, Bodil was ready. Together, they moved through the shadows, creeping up behind the guards. Ulf grabbed the first, snapping his neck in one quick twist. Bodil snuck up on the other guard from behind, grabbed a knife from his side, and sliced his throat before he could make a noise to alert the others.

Ulf was amazed by how gracefully, yet deadly, she moved. He took a step back and watched as she made her way through the camp, killing troops while they slept. The plan had been perfect. They could sneak by unnoticed and avoid any real danger under the night's cover. That is until Ulf became too distracted by Bodil, and he tripped over three sleeping troops.

"Intruders!"

"You blundering oaf!" Bodil yelled at Ulf as she stole a broad sword from the man whose guts she spilled.

"Sorry," he yelled back as he raised his sword, taking down two men in one swing.

"You will be if you don't pick up the pace," Bodil teased.

Ulf turned and watched her wield her sword better than any man he knew. Lunging, she ran one man through, charging forward and impaling two men on one blade. Then, with ease, she pulled her sword free, spinning and cutting another down at the knee, flipping her sword in her hand and bringing it down through his back. Ulf watched in awe as she took down five men while he had only finished three.

"You're slacking Ulf," Bodil teased as she tossed her handheld blade through the air, barely missing Ulf's cheek as it found its target; The eye socket of a troop sneaking up behind Ulf.

"Just admiring the view," Ulf chuckled.

He wanted to show her that he *could* protect her, even though she clearly didn't need it. Fighting side by side, they finished the remainder of the troops, with Ulf claiming one more body than Bodil.

"Braggart," she laughed, wiping the blood from her brow.

"There is still one left," Ulf pointed to the commander's tent. No one had come out; Lord Thomas was still inside.

Bodil crept around the back while Ulf took the front, coving all exits in case the commander tried to flee. Then, bursting through the fabric walls, Ulf roared his arrival. The English soldier raised a shaky hand, his sword not made for someone with such a thin and untoned frame.

"Stay back, or I will run you through!" He bellowed, trying to sound frightening, but all he did was make Ulf laugh.

"I highly doubt that," came Bodil's voice from behind.

Before he could react, she brought the hilt of her sword down on his head, knocking him to the floor.

Grabbing his pounding head, the soldier picked himself up only to be knocked back down when Bodil swept his feet from under him. Settling on his knees, the soldier looked up at Bodil and Ulf, who surrounded him.

"Where are the rest of your troops?" Ulf demanded.

"These are my troops. The only ones I command anyway," came the reply.

"Lies. A Lord would have more than a dozen men," Bodil spat.

"Lord?"

"Are you not Lord William Thomas?" Bodil asked, her eyes darting to Ulf.

The soldier laughed and laughed hard, rolling onto his side until Ulf lost his temper and picked him up by his collar. Raising him high, so his toes barely touched the floor, the soldier laughed despite his predicament.

"You think me to be Lord Thomas?"

"We know you plan to help Laird MacTavish, so where are the rest of your troops?" Ulf growled.

"You know nothing. Stupid Vikings, all brawn and no brains. I am not Lord Thomas, nor is Lord Thomas heading to help that stupid Highlander. Vikings and Highlanders are all the same, a scourge that needs to be rooted out from our lands," spat the soldier.

"You better start making sense, and now!" Bodil snapped, slapping him hard around the head. "We know about the English alliance with the Highlanders. Why? What is your aim here?"

"Alliance? Ha!" the soldier began spitting at the floor, "Alliance or not, I refuse to go to battle with dirty Highlanders."

Bodil's patience began to run thin, her temper flared. This was taking far too long, and she despised the Englishman's mocking tone.

"Ulf, drop him," she said.

Ulf dropped the man to the floor without a second thought, stepping back with a grin, ready to see the woman at work. The soldier tried to scramble away, but Bodil was too fast for him. Burying her knee in his chest and pulling the knife from her boot, she quickly ripped his trousers at the seams exposing him to the night air.

"Speak or lose your cock," she boomed, letting him feel the cold steel of her blade.

He tried to struggle, but Bodil was too strong and held him fast, digging her blade a little deeper.

"I will not ask again!" she roared.

"No, please, please," he begged, making Ulf laugh.

"Fine, I will tell you. Lord Thomas is taking the bulk of his force to the Point. He seeks a treasure left by The Jarl of Denmark for the King."

"Good boy," Bodil grinned, pulling the man to his feet and tossing him towards Ulf.

"I say we kill him. He has given us what we seek," Bodil said, playing with her knife flipping it like a toy and catching it mid-air, enjoying the panicked look in the Englishman's eyes.

"I agree," Ulf smirked.

Grabbing Ulf around the neck Bodil pulled him to her, kissing him long and hard, shoving her tongue into his mouth and massaging him with hers. Ulf was speechless when she stepped back.

"You wanted to kill the last one, and I said no. So do what you need to; I will gather supplies," she smirked, offering Ulf a wink before leaving the tent.

CHAPTER 10

"We will have to ride through the night to make it to the Point in time to warn the others," Bodil said as she mounted her horse.

"Then we ride," Ulf retorted.

And so, their journey had taken a nasty turn. Lief and the others were riding into a trap, and Arne with the ship sailed towards danger. Bodil and Ulf needed to catch up now more than ever.

Their differences had now been set aside. Their goals united. United in combat and united in love. Even if such words had not been spoken, their feelings and intentions were clear. Their mission in mind, eyes on the prize, they rode as they had never ridden before. The people they care for, their brothers in arms, needed them. Bodil and Ulf were their only hope.

Riding through the night, they ignored their aching muscles. Riding through the following day, they ignored their tired eyes. The horses grew tired, but Bodil and Ulf urged them on. Even as they drew closer to the Point, with the impending danger, every step felt like a step in the opposite direction. When the ones you love face untold risk, you can't seem to run fast enough. Pushing themselves, they rode with force. Nothing and no one would get in their way.

Their journey seemed never-ending. As they rode, they were forced to slow and take cover. The woods were full of troops. How big was Lord Thomas' army? It was not like earlier when they could easily take down a dozen men. They had to be careful. It would take one troop to see them, and their plan would be ruined.

Finally, with aching joints, tired eyes, and sore muscles, wearily, they arrived at the Point. After a quick search, they found Lief and the others at an Inn. Undercover by the fog from the coast and the darkness of night, Arne arrived just in time with the ship.

"What did you find?" Lief asked.

"You are going to want to gather everyone. We need to prepare, and we don't have much time," Bodil answered.

Everyone gathered on the ship, away from prying eyes and overeager ears. They couldn't afford anyone else to know their plans or find out about the Jarl's treasure. They had a big enough force to deal with. So, Lief, Sven, Revna, Arne, Toke, Ulf, and Bodil plotted long into the night with the crew keeping watch. If the English and Highlanders thought they could steal from the Vikings, they were wrong. If they thought they could defeat the Vikings, they were wrong.

EPILOGUE

THE SUN HAD NOT YET RISEN over the horizon. But the sky was beginning to show the first signs of light. Overnight, the fog from the sea had thickened and travelled far onto land. With Bodil and Ulf's help, the group plotted the troop's approach point through the trees. Lief had insisted on Ulf and Bodil sitting this battle out. They had done enough for them over the last few days. Ulf and Bodil both argued against that. This fight was just as much theirs as anyone else's. But since Ulf was falling asleep while they discussed strategy, Lief had made the decision for them.

"You rode for a day and a night; you need rest," Lief insisted.

"We can fight," Bodil fought back.

"I do not doubt your skills. Yours or Ulf's, but your journey has taken its toll. You risk injury. I cannot split forces to take care of you both if you become injured. Rest on the ship; trust we can handle it," Lief said.

"But...." Ulf started, but Coline interjected.

"We would be lost if not for you two. Trust us, it is our time to protect you now," Coline smiled.

Reluctantly, Ulf and Bodil stood aboard the ship watching their brothers and sisters in arms ride out into the dawn to face the English troops.

"I didn't come all this way to not join in the fight," Bodil complained, "what am I supposed to do now?"

"I suppose we do as instructed and get some rest," Ulf sighed, heading off to his cabin.

Bodil watched him leave feeling somewhat disappointed. They were finally alone, with nothing to do. Despite their long journey, fighting the English troops and everything with MacTavish, Bodil was full of energy. Pent up tension and unanswered questions. Frustration built between her legs. They had shared several moments, and she was not going to sleep without getting answers.

Bodil stood outside Ulf's door for longer than intended; she knew what she wanted to do and say but suddenly found her nerve had gone. Pull yourself together, she told herself as she reached for the door handle. Ulf lay on the bed. His clothes lay strewn on the floor next to him, the wool blanket was the only thing covering him from the waist down.

Seeing him like that made Bodil's mind go blank. Everything she had planned on saying vanished from her thoughts. Actions speak louder than words, she thought. Closing the door behind her with more force than needed was enough to alert Ulf to her presence.

"Everything alright?" he asked as he sat upright.

Bodil didn't say a word. Slowly, she began to take off her clothes, keeping her eyes locked with his. With each item she removed, Ulf's eyes grew darker. Her pulse quickened as his eyes filled with lust, and his tongue ran across his lips. Finally, standing before him naked, she expected to feel nervous. Instead, she felt empowered and beautiful. She was a little taller than Ulf, but not by much. She stood, letting him take in the sight of her wide hips, strong muscular legs, and full round bosom.

"We are alone. We have no way of knowing how the battle against the English and Highlanders is going. The others may not return, and death could come for us by nightfall. All we have is now, and we left a lot unfinished from MacTavish's castle…. I'm a woman who always finishes what she starts…." Bodil breathed, taking slow steps towards him.

"Stand up," she ordered, and Ulf obliged.

Letting the blanket fall to his feet, revealing the body she hadn't been able to get out of her mind. Ulf stood and let Bodil's eyes roam over him from head to toe. He sucked in a breath as she trailed her hands over his firm pecks and shoulders. Bodil had a thing for shoulders; it was a sign of strength, and Ulf's shoulders made her weak.

"Sit down," she ordered; mesmerised by her take-charge attitude, Ulf said nothing as he sat on the bed, letting his hands glide over her hips and around to her high, firm backside.

Bodil climbed on top of him, setting her hips wide as she straddled across his lap. Ulf's hands ran up her back and into her hair as he pulled her face down to his.

"Are you sure about this?" he whispered, hoping she wouldn't back out now. He had started to honestly care for her. And while his cock ached to feel her, he only wanted to be with her if she genuinely wanted to.

"I've never been this sure of anything," she answered, kissing him gently, waiting for his reaction.

He opened his mouth, welcoming her, their tongues dancing, fighting with passion. Bodil reached down and took him in her hand, guiding him inside her. All the waiting had her dripping her juices all over him, resulting in a satisfied groan as he filled her.

He had more girth than Grom, and she loved how Ulf filled every part of her. She began to slide herself up and down his length, slowly at first, keeping her eyes on his, watching the passion building in his eyes. The slow speed was torture for them both. Bodil needed to feel more, she picked up her pace, and Ulf cupped her buttocks, helping her rise and fall, panting and growling with each movement.

Bodil clawed at his back as she felt the pressure between her legs building, growing stronger as the smell of their sweat and sex filled the air. Bodil moaned in Ulf's ear as he flicked his tongue over her nipples, the sensation adding to her building ecstasy. Finally, it was becoming too much to take, and she screamed his name as she came apart around him. She arched her back and clenched herself around Ulf, making him groan and moan as she shook, waves rolling through every part of her body, relieving the ache in her muscles.

Her legs shook under her, her muscles dancing. She looked back at

Ulf, who grinned back at her, his eyes glazed with desire. Bodil climbed down and knelt between Ulf's legs, her hands gliding over his thighs, keeping her eyes on his. She lowered herself and took him in her mouth, tasting the results of her pleasure that glistened over him. Ulf let his head fall back as he gasped at the feel of her mouth around him, the way her tongue rolled and teased. Then, resting a hand on the back of her head, he bucked his hips, his own ecstasy not far away.

"By the gods, woman," he groaned, his breath coming short and fast.

Bodil moaned deep in her throat; the vibrations rolling from her to Ulf were enough to send him over the edge as he filled her mouth with his own pleasure. Bodil swallowed him down and licked her lips as she rose to her feet, her legs still shaking under her.

"You are something else, woman," Ulf chuckled.

Not giving her a chance to respond, he stood and wrapped her arms around his hips and laid her down on the bed beneath him. Ulf could taste them both as he kissed her lips, kissing her until they were both breathless. His beard tickled her chest as he ran his mouth down her neck, collar bone, and across her chest. Taking her breast in his mouth, Bodil moaned. Her moans grew as he spread her legs wide, rolling his fingers over her, teasing her until her pleasure began to build again. Bodil stifled a chuckle as his beard tickled her belly while he travelled his kisses down between her breasts to her stomach, to her hips until his face was in between her thighs.

Bodil looked down to see Ulf giving her the same carnal, primal desire-filled glare she had offered him. Eyes locked, he turned his neck, teasing her as he kissed her inner thigh, making her jump and groan as he gently nipped her thigh, leaving minor red marks behind.

"I'm not going to stop until I hear your voice scream my name to reach every part of this ship," Ulf said, his voice was a low, deep tone of danger and pleasure.

Ulf pushed her thighs wider apart, rolling his nose through the small patch of dark hair. His tongue began with slow teasing licks, tormenting Bodil until she felt she couldn't take anymore. Every time she felt herself about to erupt, Ulf would stop. It was maddening but in the best possible way.

"Ulf, please," she whispered.

"What did you say?" he asked a smirk of pleasure across his lips.

"Please, Ulf, I can't take much more teasing. I need you too...."

"Make you scream my name?"

"Yes, by the gods and all of Asgärd, yes!" she cried.

Ulf slipped two thick fingers inside her, curving them and stroking her insides at a slow tantalising pace as his tongue danced over the sensitive bud that screamed for release. Bodil panted and gasped, her hands running through Ulf's hair, keeping him in place.

"Ulf..." Bodil whispered.

"Louder," he spoke against her, the vibrations from his deep voice sending waves through her.

Tension built in her stomach as she moaned his name, only to be met with another chorus of "louder" each time she moaned.

"Oh gods, Ulf!" she screamed, tethered on the edge of glory.

Finally, Ulf allowed her the release she begged for, wrapping his mouth around her, sucking her aching bud, and sending Bodil falling deep into a realm of ecstasy she had never felt before. He sucked harder as her hips bucked until he could taste her pleasure on his tongue.

"I'm not done with you yet," he grinned, crawling up her as she panted for air.

"Do with me what you will; I'm having far too much fun to stop now," Bodil grinned.

THE END

AILSA
TRACKING THE KING'S RAIDERS

PROLOGUE

So FAR, the trip to the Point had been unsuccessful, a total failure. The locals refused to talk, avoiding the Vikings at every opportunity, some even spitting in their direction. To make matters worse, Ulf and Bodil arrived with news of an oncoming attack. Morning approached, leaving Leif with not much time to rest. Leif gathered the others and made a plan for the morning. Coline was to stay in the inn as her leg still needed to heal. Ulf and Bodil were not happy about being ordered to sit this battle out, but Leif knew it was for the best.

After their talk, the group prepared for battle, but Leif could barely think. He needed time to himself. His mind raced, and self-doubt crept in. He wasn't feeling much like a leader; the entire mission had been a mess from the start. They were no closer to finding the Jarl's stash and were quickly running out of leads.

Leif was used to being away from home. Expeditions were what he lived for. Something about this expedition felt different. For the first time, loneliness was becoming his uninvited friend. Seeing his comrades, all finding love only amplified his pain. He had never worried about finding someone. Love had not been something he had looked for, but loneliness is a cruel emotion. Looking over at his crew, hearing them laugh, and seeing the women wrapped in his men's arms made his skin itch. Restless and frustrated, he decided to take a walk to clear his head.

Leif always felt best by the sea. The sea represented freedom, endless possibilities, and adventure. Travelling by land for as long as he had on this latest mission didn't help with how he was feeling now. As the sound of the waves called his name, he couldn't shake the feeling that someone, or something, was travelling with him. Loneliness was playing tricks on him.

The sky grew dense with fog. And the air felt close, the way it always did before a storm. The waves crashed against the shore. Leif picked the perfect spot to admire the sea. A rock jutted out from the cliff's edge, creating a balcony over the water. The moon's reflection danced on the water. The sound of the waves was like a song to his ears, a lullaby that soothed him.

"I only want to do the right thing. Protect my men, fulfil my orders to the King, and protect my country. When did this expedition become so difficult?" Leif spoke to himself. Or to the gods? To the sea? He didn't know. But it had helped.

"A war? It would be useless. Countless innocents would die, and for what? Coin? It's senseless. I must think of my family and my friends. How can I best prevent the worst? Please guide my hand in battle and help me lead my men well," Leif sighed, standing and watching the waves.

The horizon slowly grew lighter as dawn approached. But the sun wouldn't show its face for a few more hours. Leif turned, deciding that even though he knew he wasn't going to get much sleep if any, it was time to return to the inn. Leif could feel a presence. Was it a guiding hand of the gods answering his prayer? He didn't know.

As he approached the inn, he was unaware of the shadow that followed close behind.

CHAPTER 1

AILSA MCCANNON PACED the shadows of the inn. Dawn was still a few hours off; the rain that had been holding out had now started. A soft drizzle. The sound was soothing to the ear and calming to the soul. The Viking she had been following had returned to his room a while ago, and she still had no idea what to do next.

She had been debating what to do ever since the Vikings arrived in her village. She had a history with Vikings. But something inside her shifted after she overheard this one talking to the waves out on the rock's edge. Replaying his words repeatedly in her mind, resting her head back against the wall and allowing the gentle flow of the rain-drops to tickle her face, she decided what to do.

Slipping around the side of the inn, she crept inside. The side door was rarely locked, and she was happy to see that this was the case yet again. The entrance opened up into the hallway just under the stairs, tucked away behind another door that led to the dining hall. She could still hear the soft rumble of one or two residents drinking and conversing.

All the rooms upstairs were occupied. When she was outside, she noted which window held light when her Viking arrived. Closing her eyes, she followed her internal map of the layout of the inn. Once she was sure that she had the right door, she reached into her pocket and pulled out her trusted tools to pick the lock.

One wrong move or one loud turn of the lock, she would be surrounded. If one of this Viking's comrades chose to take an early morning stroll, she would be caught red-handed. Breathing deeply, she steadied her shaking hands as her heart beat deep in her throat. She prayed to all the gods that she was doing the right thing as she slowly, quietly slipped inside.

Gently closing the door behind her, she surveyed the room. All seemed well. The candle by the window cast a soft dancing light across the room. From the shadows, she assumed the Viking slept on his straw-covered bed. She had been in that room before; she knew which floorboards creaked and cracked. Taking a slow step to the left, heading around the bed, she knew it was too late.

Immediately, the Viking jumped from the shadows grabbing her from behind and tossing her onto the bed. She flipped herself over, preparing to fight back, but she was far too slow; he covered her body with his, and held his knife to her throat.

"Who are you? Why have you been following me?" he demanded.

CHAPTER 2

LEIF HAD WAITED for longer than expected for the one following him to make their move. He had noticed their presence the moment he left the water's edge. When he felt their presence and heard the subtle footsteps, he had expected his follower to be a man, a troop scouting for the English. Now, as Leif straddled his attacker, he was surprised to find his blade at the throat of a beautiful woman.

As it always did when in the presence of such beauty, his body reacted of its own accord. It had been far too long since he felt the tender touch, loving embrace, and warmth of a woman's body beneath him. Yet, he couldn't let himself be distracted even for a moment. She was still a threat. And he needed answers.

She was more intelligent than he had given her credit for. In the moments it took him to register his body's response, he had allowed himself to become distracted, and she noticed, instantly taking advantage. Seeing a woman beneath him, he moved his blade away from her throat, giving her enough room to slip her arm around his. She pushed against him, flipping him over and off the bed. She leapt to her feet and ran for the door. Leif tried to grab her leg to stop her, but she was too agile. Leif was determined not to be outwitted by this intruder. She still had questions to answer.

Leif jumped to his feet, launching himself over the other side of the bed, making it to the door before her. By the look of astonishment on her face, Leif could tell that he was a much better warrior than she expected. Taking a page from her book, he used her moment's distraction to his advantage.

Grabbing her and spinning her around so she couldn't see his next move, aware that others could be alerted to their struggle, he clasped his hand over her mouth. She struggled against his grasp, but Leif was much stronger than her, and her struggles only tightened his grip. She was a fighter, strong and defined. Leif allowed his hands to roam a little, freely admiring the tone and muscles of her body, the smoothness of her skin, and how she felt in his arms. Quickly snapping himself from his distraction, he tightened his grip.

"Do not make a sound. If you promise not to scream, I will offer my name to show you I mean you no ill will. I am the one they call Leif. I will let you go, but only once you have answered my questions. Nod if you understand," Leif growled down her ear.

The woman in his arms stopped struggling against him, gently nodding her agreement. Slowly Leif removed his hand.

"Who are you, and why are you here?" Leif asked.

"I'm a whore; I simply have the wrong room. I'm sorry for disturbing you. Now please can I leave before my patron thinks I have changed my mind," Ailsa replied.

Pretending to be a woman who sells her body was an excuse Leif hadn't heard before. He admired her bravado, but Leif was no fool. The rest of the rooms in the inn were occupied by his men, and they all had a woman in their beds.

"Nice try. My men occupy the rest of this inn, and none of them sleep alone. I also have never seen a whore who dresses ready for a fight or who can pick a lock," Leif replied.

"You flatter me. I dress how I do to appease the Danes who have taken these lands. I was hired to warm the bed of a pair. Have you never experienced such a thing before? Perhaps when I am done, I can call on one of my friends, and we can show you," she whispered, moving her hips against him, feeling his response.

"Try again. Whoring was outlawed in my country years ago. We do not participate in such activities. When a Dane is with a woman, she is there of her own free will, not because she is being paid," Leif argued.

"Respectfully, you are not in Denmark. You are on the shores of England. Perhaps your men want to try local customs," Ailsa argued back.

Leif laughed low and deep down her ear. She was not as good a liar as she thought, but he liked how she insisted on sticking with her lie and how she rolled her hips in an attempt to convince him.

"I am a patient man, but you are pushing my last nerve. I told you that I would not harm you, and I intend to keep my word. All I ask is that you tell me the truth. I will not ask again. Who are you? And why are you following me?" Leif demanded.

Sighing deeply, the woman relaxed against Leif's grip. "My name is Ailsa McCannon, and all I seek is answers too."

"Answers to what?" Leif asked softly.

Reaching into her dress, Ailsa pulled out a long silver chain from around her neck. Dangling from the chain was a small broch, one that was usually worn by a man to hold his cloak. Leif reached for it, holding it closer to the candle's light for a better view. On inspection, he could tell it was Danish.

"Where did you get this?" Leif asked, realising he had seen that same broch before.

"It belonged to my father," Ailsa answered.

CHAPTER 3

THIS WAS the last thing Leif expected, or needed, on the eve of battle. Releasing Ailsa, he unclipped the broch, lighting another candle to get a better view of it. Studying the pin, Ailsa hovered nearby, clearly nervous that she wouldn't be given the pin back. Leif was now surer than ever, based on the workmanship, material, and decoration, that he knew the pin.

"I know this artistry. It belongs to those in direct service to the King," Leif said.

Leif reached for the table by the dresser. He picked up his own, showing it to Ailsa. The two pins were nearly identical, whereas Leif's was much newer. Ailsa tentatively took them from him, examining them closely, mumbling something to herself that Leif couldn't hear. He was watching her closely under the candle's light. That's when he noticed it.

He saw her reddish-blonde hair for the first time and how her accent had changed when she spoke Danish. She was a Highlander but also a Dane.

"I'm sorry I can't help you out further. These pins are common enough. And from your age, I don't think I would know who it could have belonged to," Leif took back his pin.

"If you have one too, surely you must know of others who served the King in the past. Is there not one name you can think of who travelled to these shores before returning home?" Ailsa asked.

"I'm sorry. Many raided these coasts long before the settlement was established. But I know little of one who might have left his pin…. or a baby behind," Leif gently shook his head.

Ailsa looked almost tearful; she held onto so much hope that she could finally be getting the answers she longed for. Catching Leif staring, she drew herself up, her face instantly hardening.

"Thank you; I apologise for being a trouble. Good night," Ailsa nodded, turning to leave.

Leif felt for her tears. He recognised the courage it had taken her to confront someone from his group. Leif and his men were tall, muscular, and some of the fiercest warriors in the King's service; their sight was often intimidating. Thinking over the animosity that he and his men had received since arriving at the Point also gave Ailsa extra points for bravery.

"I bid you pause, Ailsa. I admire your courage, considering the bad blood between Vikings and Highlanders. I'm always willing to learn. Would you care to explain how you came across such courage?" Leif enquired.

She paused at the door, her face was still as hard as a rock, and she only slightly turned to face him.

"The men who were here before you were cruel…." Ailsa answered.

"The Jarl's men?" asked Leif.

Ailsa nodded but didn't offer any other details; it was evident to Leif it was a subject she didn't care to elaborate on.

"So, if the Jarl's men were so cruel, why did you feel safe enough following me? I could be just as cruel for all you know."

Ailsa offered a small smile that barely touched her lips.

"You are not a cruel man. A man who prays to the gods so earnestly before battle, praying for guidance to do the right thing, is a good man. I know that much," she offered, slipping out the door.

CHAPTER 4

AILSA BEGAN TO HEAD HOME, to the home she shared with her mother. A private little space that had been forgotten about by the local villages, a place that offered her safety and privacy. Ailsa tried to keep her mother in mind, as she walked towards the middle of the village; she did everything she did to help her mother.

Yet, the further away from the Viking she walked, the more her body remembered his touch. When he had held her tightly to him, his hands had roamed. Though he hadn't intended to, his fingers had slipped below her neckline, stroking her breasts. Her skin still tingled at the memory.

She could still feel his weight on top of her, controlling her and hovering above her. Even as her mind remembered how his body reacted to her being beneath him, she didn't care that he held a knife to her throat. Though intimidating, she felt no threat, as though he would never harm her.

The way his breath stroked her neck, the deep growl in her ear as he spoke to her. She could still smell his scent on her clothes.

Stopping in her tracks, she allowed her hands to roam over the places his fingers had touched. Grabbing her collar and lifting it to her nose, she inhaled his scent deeply. It sent a shiver down her spine. Ailsa couldn't remember when her body had responded to a man in such a way. With a yearning in her stomach, she wanted to go back to him. Ailsa wouldn't know what to say when she got there. She smiled to herself at the memory of him seeing through her lies. How had she ever thought that she could convince him she was a whore? He was far too clever for that.

He had been so gentle with her. He could have been more forceful, more dangerous. He was not like the other Vikings she had encountered. He was taller, with arms as big as tree trunks; she remembered the feel of his chest against her back, the way his hips had involuntarily pressed closer into her. Leif. The way he almost growled his name, its sound on her ear. She wondered how it would feel rolling off her tongue in the throes of ecstasy.

She stood, allowing these thoughts to distract her when a rider galloped into the village. Startled, she hid in the shadows watching and following close by. She didn't recognise the rider. He wore all black with no identifying banners, the hood of his cloak pulled far down, hiding his face. It was far too close to dawn for someone to be riding into the village with such urgency. Something was amiss.

Ailsa crept through the shadows, staying far enough back that the rider wouldn't see her but close enough that she wouldn't lose sight. Finally, the rider stopped outside the Chief's home.

Who could be calling on the Chief at such an hour? Ailsa thought.

Sneaking past the rider's horse, she made an extra effort not to spook him lest he alert his rider to her presence. Tiptoeing around the house, she searched for a way to sneak inside. Voices alerted her to the rider conversing with the mayor. Panicked, she dropped into a crouch under the window and listened.

"Your information proved invaluable," said one voice.

"Glad I could be of service. When will the rest of your forces get here?" Urged the other voice that Ailsa recognised as the mayor.

"They will be here shortly Do not worry, Sire. This Viking scum will no longer be a concern for your village."

Ailsa stayed in the shadows and waited for the rider to leave. She watched as he rode out of the village. First, she tried to figure out what the rider had meant. Then, thinking back to the inn, she realised something; it was a fact that had her trembling with dread twisting in the pit of her stomach.

The inn was eerily quiet. All of the other times she had crept inside, it was abuzz with life. People either gathered in the dining hall or the bar. People usually gathered in and around, yet there had been not a soul in sight.

It was empty. The inn is never empty. Travellers and locals usually filled this place. Where was everyone? Who was the rider? Ailsa questioned herself. *It's a trap!*

Ailsa didn't know why because she didn't even know the Viking, but she couldn't just sit back knowing what she knew. Instinct kicked in, and she took off back towards the inn. She had to warn Leif.

CHAPTER 5

LEIF HAD A HIDDEN POWER; it was the same power that alerted him when he was being followed. He never knew what caused this feeling, a twist in his gut, a twitch of the ear, or a change of the wind, but he always trusted his gut when he got that feeling. Right then, his gut was telling him that he and his men had fallen into a trap.

He thought about it objectively. They had stayed at several inns during their travels, just like the one he found himself in that night. So many inns he had lost count, but they all had one thing in common. No matter what time of night, they were all busy with life. That night, the inn was far too quiet; even as he travelled back from the shore, he hadn't spotted a soul.

He had left Revna and Toke on guard. Nothing got past them, so how had Ailsa managed to get by them? The inn was small. There were not many places to hide. From the door of his room, he had a clear view of the entire second floor; there was no way she could have gotten by unnoticed.

As he tried to figure it out, he heard someone outside his door. Leif blew out the candles sending the room into darkness. Then, with his knife drawn, he stood behind the door, waiting for his intruder. The door slowly opened, and a figure stepped past the threshold. Immediately, he grabbed the figure and slammed it against the door, closing it with a bang.

"Don't say a word. Move, and I will slit your throat!" Leif growled low.

His hands roamed over the person under his control. Curves, toned muscles, a pert buttock. Curves he recognised. His hands roamed higher, searching for a weapon. Breast? He had an idea of who it was, yet he couldn't bring himself to stop pawing at her. His skin prickled as he heard her breathing become heavier.

"Ailsa?" he asked into the darkness.

"Do you know any other whores who can pick locks?" she joked.

"I think we have established that you are not a whore."

"But I could be," she teased, "I seem to keep finding my way into your arms....or pinned under you."

Leif said nothing, momently stunned by her whit. He wasn't one to smile often but was glad for the room's darkness so she couldn't see his face or how he struggled to contain his laugh.

"Is that an axe at your hip, or are you just pleased to see me again?" she joked again.

Leif couldn't ignore how his body always seemed to respond to her. Her whit was now becoming a problem; her words and what they insinuated also had an effect. Leif was lost for words but also couldn't bring himself to pull away from her. Ailsa fell silent, their breathing being the only sound in the room.

"If you stopped breaking into my room, perhaps you wouldn't end up in my arms," Leif finally spoke, his voice hoarse.

"Now, where is the fun in that?" Ailsa hummed, rocking her hips in response, mimicking her actions from earlier that evening.

"If I didn't know any better, I would say you are trying to get your-self in trouble," Leif whispered.

Trouble! The word forced Leif to remember where his mind had been before Ailsa arrived.

He lowered his knife once again, tucking it safely into his belt.

"Why did you come back?"

"A rider rode into town. I overheard a conversation. You and your men are in a trap," Ailsa gasped, remembering why she had run back with such haste.

"Wake the others, be silent about it. No candles; do not alert anyone who may be waiting that we are awake," Leif ordered.

"What will you do?"

"I left two of my best on guard. I began to question how you managed to slip by them."

"I saw no guards either time I broke in."

"I shall go look for them. Be cautious in waking the others. If an attack is imminent, we must act fast."

Ailsa slipped from the room while Leif watched. His gut twisted once more, causing his heart to ache as doubts about her sprang up in his mind. How was she allowed to pass so easily? What if she was a spy for the English? Or, worse, what if the Highlanders and the English had once again joined forces?

His doubts eased a little when he remembered that she had no weapon. She had spent most of their acquaintance in his arms or underneath him, plus his hands had roamed all over her when they first met. If she had a weapon, she would have drawn it, or he would have felt the outline of it, close as they were. He didn't think she could or would harm anyone, she had the opportunity to hurt him when she tossed him off the bed, but still, suspicion lay heavy on the air.

As Ailsa slowly woke the others, Leif headed downstairs in search of Toke and Revna. The suspicion towards Ailsa grew stronger when he made his way to the back of the tavern to find Revna unconscious on the floor; blood was matted to a small section of her hair. Toke was nowhere to be seen. He checked Revna over and was relieved to find her injury wasn't too bad. She would recover, and may the gods help whoever attacked her, for they would feel the full force of her wrath.

CHAPTER 6

THE OTHERS WERE CONFUSED about who Ailsa was, but hearing Leif had sent her, they followed her command. Leif ordered a search of the inn. Unfortunately, whoever had taken Toke had left no trail. No struggle, no footprints; it was eerie.

Revna finally came to, brushing off her brother, Sven, who insisted on fawning over her like she was a child.

"I told you I am fine! Just wait until I find out who did this. I'm going to bring down the full force of the Valkyrie down on their heads!" Revna raged, spitting madness.

"Calm down, or you will alert whoever awaits us," Sven hushed.

"Let them come! I want them to come so I can tear their spines out and crush a few skulls. If Toke is harmed in any way, the Red Blood King will be nothing compared to what chaos I break loose," Revna continued to rage.

"Red Blood King?" Ailsa whispered to Leif.

"A King from legend, he was known for being driven mad with blood lust. He killed so many his own men had to take him down to stop him," Leif answered.

Revna paced back and forth; no one could calm her down. Her eyes burned deep into Ailsa, and Ailsa knew she didn't trust her.

"What can you remember?" Sven asked.

"Nothing! Whoever it was that snuck up on me and bashed me over the head!" Revna spat.

"What do you think happened to Toke? There are no signs of a struggle. Do you think he followed whoever attacked you?" Ulf asked.

"What if he was taken? They could have used you for blackmail," Ailsa nodded towards Revna.

"Come again?" Revna snarled, stopping in her tracks, her hands balled into fists at her side.

"If they thought he cared, perhaps they told him he had to go, or they would hurt you," Ailsa gulped, suddenly nervous under the raging fury of Revna's gaze.

"And who exactly are you?" Revna asked, taking slow steps towards Ailsa.

"My name is Ailsa McCannon...."

"And why are you here?" Revna growled.

"Enough, Revna, we do not have time for this," Leif warned.

It took a few moments for Revna to relax, but she obeyed Leif's command, still keeping a close eye on Ailsa.

"I suggest we leave this inn before dawn. Use the cover of darkness to escape."

"What part of *us* involves *you*?" Revna snapped.

"Why should we leave? We are not going anywhere without Toke," Sven said.

"I can't help but think it's odd how this one appears to know a lot about what goes on around here, yet we know nothing about you," Ulf grumbled.

The group slowly began to close in around Ailsa, creating a wall she knew she had no hope of getting past.

"Why are you so eager for us to leave? Why so eager for us to leave behind our brother in arms? Do you make a habit of abandoning your own people?" Arne interjected.

Ailsa looked to Leif for help, but his own suspicion grew as the others rained down their questions. What Ailsa expected to see in his eyes was sympathy or compassion. She had come back to warn him after all. Yet all she saw was a stone wall, hiding anything that may have laid there before.

"How are you able to get in and out of the inn so easily? You managed to get by two of our best," Arne glared.

"No one was on guard when I arrived. No one ever sees me; I'm invisible," Ailsa replied. "I've lived in the village all my life. When you spend enough time in one place, you notice people's comings and goings. The inn isn't too big; it's easy to get in and out unnoticed," Ailsa rambled.

"I don't believe a word she is saying. I think she's a spy," Sven growled.

"No! No! I'm not!" Ailsa panicked suddenly, feeling like she couldn't breathe surrounded by such mighty warriors with no escape and no way to defend herself.

"My door was locked when you first arrived. Yet, you managed to unlock it twice, even bragged about your lock-picking abilities just moments ago," Leif said.

Ailsa scanned the faces that stared down at her, all a mix of surprise, suspicion, and anger. For the first time, she felt she was in danger, and the only way out was the truth.

"Okay, fine, I yield. I may be something of a.... thief. I have had no choice, it's not something I am proud of, but I do what I can to survive. It's the only way I have known how to survive since I was as young as I could walk. I'm very good at getting in and out of places unseen. I followed you when you got into town, and none of you noticed.... Well, except Leif tonight," Ailsa confessed, concerned she may have done more harm than good by speaking the truth.

"Great, a thief. Worse than a spy. We cannot trust her!" Revna snapped, trying to force herself through the group to Ailsa, but Sven and Ulf held her back.

"I agree with Revna. However, our mission is far too important. We have risked far too much to risk having a thief in our midst," Arne warned.

Ailsa looked over to Leif with pleading eyes. Begging for help. Leif watched her carefully when a thought occurred to him.

"She may still prove of use to us. If she can get in and out unnoticed, she can also show us how. Once outside, we can do a proper search for Toke, find him, and plan out our attack," Leif offered.

The group argued amongst themselves; none trusted Ailsa, especially with the Jarl's hoard at stake.

"Enough! I am the commander here! You do not have to trust her, but you have to trust me and obey my orders!" Leif growled, silencing the group.

"Ailsa, prove to me that my judgement is not misplaced. Take Coline to safety," Leif said.

"I will go with her! Just to be safe," Bodil stepped forward. "I was sworn to protect her, and until this mission is complete, I intend to keep that promise."

Ulf straightened his eyes, beaming with pride for his woman. Arne relaxed a little, knowing that Bodil would protect Coline; he hadn't liked the idea of Ailsa leaving with Coline, especially with her leg still healing.

CHAPTER 7

"Follow me," Ailsa said, heading down and out of the inn.

None of the group attempted to move; everyone shared a look, waiting to see their comrade's reaction. All then looked to Leif. Leif rolled his eyes and followed Ailsa, swiftly followed by the rest of his crew.

Sneaking out of the inn had proven the easy part. Getting the others to trust she was not leading them into a trap was another task entirely. Outside the inn, Ailsa led them around the back of the barn used for supplies. It was the quickest and easiest way to access the village without being seen.

Past the inn, the village was tightly packed with huts of different sizes and shapes. Over the years, people from other villages had migrated to the Point, and the village had grown swiftly. No one had expected it to grow as it did. As a result, the houses were packed closely together, creating a labyrinth around the village square.

Teaching the Vikings to move quietly and not alert the inhabitants was no small feat. Getting them to fit through between the others was even more difficult. Thyra and Revna lead the group, while they were built more considerably than the average woman, they still made an easy enough task of manoeuvring the small spaces, giving the others behind a clear view of the best track to take.

"This is ridiculous. Why are we sneaking around like children?" Ulf complained.

"Because we do not know if your enemy is combing the village to find you, and for the ninth time, be quiet!" Ailsa replied.

She and Leif followed the group from the back, wedged between the tight gaps between homes and Leif and Arne. Ailsa had never felt so trapped before, yet safe at the same time. It was an odd feeling that she didn't know how to process.

"The village square is right up ahead. So, you will be able to move more freely there. From there, it's a lot easier to get to the shoreline," Ailsa insisted.

Crackling, banging, and the smell of smoke caught Leif and Ailsa's attention. Turning to look back the way they came, Leif's eyes widened. Ailsa had been right, they were in a trap, and if they had stayed to argue any longer, they might not have made it out alive. They watched as the inn erupted into flames.

"Halt! look," Leif ordered.

"By the gods," Ulf gasped.

The group stopped to examine the scene; even from a distance between the inn and the square, figures were visible moving against the flames. Armed soldiers guarded every exit, waiting for anyone who could be trying to escape.

"They still think we are inside," Revna whispered.

"They are waiting for a fight," Sven retorted with glee and mischief in his voice.

"Then let's give them what they came for," Thyra spoke.

Ailsa stood frozen with alarm. Looking over to the flames, there was a small army of at least twenty. Their group only consisted of seven, including herself, and she was no fighter.

"You can't be thinking of going back?" she asked.

"Why not?" Revna snapped.

"You are outnumbered, there are at least twenty, and that's just the soldiers we can see. Who knows how many more they have lying in wait," Ailsa panicked.

"We have taken down far bigger forces with far fewer men, plus they are distracted searching for us. So, let's not leave them disappointed. Don't worry, our little pickpocket. We are not asking you to fight," Ulf said.

Ailsa looked over to Leif, her eyes begging for him to see reason, but she knew it was a lost cause. He, too, shared the group's thoughts, and anger boiled in his eyes.

"We have taken down much greater forces. Ailsa, you stay here. Everyone else, follow me. Let's show these fools what happens when you underestimate Vikings," Leif commanded.

Ailsa watched in astonishment as the group pushed past her, pulling out their weapons, and travelling back towards the flames.

CHAPTER 8

AILSA WATCHED as the group headed back to the inn. She debated leaving, which would make the Vikings even more suspicious that she was hiding something. Finally, after several minutes of thought, Ailsa followed the group but stayed far enough behind to not get involved. Concealed in the shadows, she watched as the group moved silently, creeping around in the shadows the way she had taught them only moments before. Her moment of subtle pride passed quickly when she heard a soft gurgling sound from her left. Following the sound, she watched as Thyra grabbed a soldier from behind and slit his throat before he could alert the others.

Ailsa's eyes drifted further to see Revna bury her axe in a man's skull. The Vikings got through many men as silently as they could before one of the British troops came upon them, alerting his comrades with a yell.

Suddenly, all the troops gathered around them in an effort to trap the Vikings. Ailsa was both amazed, impressed, and horrified at the Viking's skills. She had met Vikings before, but none had moved with the fluidity, grace, and accuracy that these ones did.

Ulf took down three men by impaling two on his broadsword and flinging his axe into the face of another. Arne and Revna battled six troops, making a mockery of them, taunting them before cutting them down. Sven hadn't left Thyra's side; Ailsa had quickly deduced that she was his woman and he, her man. It was clear that Thyra didn't need Sven to protect her. She was just as powerful and cunning, even stopping mid-battle for a quick adrenaline-filled kiss before she cut a man's head clean off his neck as he went after Sven.

Ailsa was fascinated with their skills, confidence, and how easily they took down so many soldiers. Ailsa was a skilled thief and had a talent for getting in and out of anywhere unnoticed, yet she had never had the need nor the instruction on how to take care of herself in battle. She hoped that Revna would warm to her enough to teach her at some point. With Revna and Thyra's fighting skills and her ability to become one with the shadows, she would be unstoppable.

To her surprise, she found the adrenaline, fear, and blood lust oddly titillating. Her breath quickened, her pulse raced, and unknowingly, her hands drifted down her body. Then, feeling her nipples strain under her touch, her eyes drifted to the last person whose hands had been there; Leif.

Was it the intoxicating rush of a battle? Or was it that he had been so kind to her when the others had scared her half to death? She didn't know. But one thing she did know was that as the battle raged on, her heart fought for Leif's safety.

Just then, a large man with a round belly and grey hair who looked far too old and unfit to be in battle charged at Leif. Ailsa assumed that he was the British commander from his armour and the cloak on his back. Leif sidestepped, avoiding the attack and slicing the gut of a man who approached from the other side.

"Over here! They are over here!" Came a scream from the other side of the tavern.

Ailsa looked and a team of troops ran round to join the fight; a line of four archers ignited their arrows with flames. Fear and dread filled Ailsa. She wanted to help but knew she would likely be captured, killed or worse, get someone else killed in her effort. As the battle raged, she thought again about leaving but couldn't pull herself away until she knew Leif was safe.

Men cried out in pain as they were shoved into the flames. Thyra had made quick work of the archers while the others finished off the remainder of the troops. Ailsa was impressed. Being so vastly outnumbered, she had thought the Vikings stupid, letting their emotions get their better; instead, they had triumphed.

"They will think twice about trying to make fools of us again," Ulf cheered.

The overly plump British commander continued to try and fight Leif, who danced out of his way at every attack, laughing and mocking his foolishness until the man was too tired even to lift his sword. Then, panting, red-faced and sweating from the heat of the flames that still raged on behind him, the commander stopped fighting. But, putting on his bravest face in front of the Vikings, even Ailsa knew it was a front, and the man was trembling.

"This? This is the best the British have to offer? I'm insulted that they sent this pig of a man to try and kill us. What would be the honour in dying at his hand?" Leif growled, grabbing the man by the collar.

Lifting the man with ease to the point his toes barely scraped on the floor, Leif demanded answers, firing question after question at him. The man squirmed in Leif's grasp, shaking his head and refusing to answer.

"Where is Toke? What did your men do with him?" roared Revna.

Ailsa heard the rumble of hooves, and her head snapped around in the direction of the sound. Reinforcements were coming, and there was a lot more than the previous batch. Ailsa's heart leapt up into her throat. She knew that she must act. Jumping from the shadows, much to the surprise of most of the group, she barged past Revna, who tried to get in her way, making a beeline to Leif.

Grabbing his shoulder, she tried to get his attention, but his anger burned into the man, slowly turning purple under his grasp.

"We have to go. Reinforcements are coming," Ailsa insisted.

"I need answers," Leif snarled.

"And you will get them, but not here; we have to go," Ailsa insisted harder, tugging on his shoulder to no avail.

"She's right, horses, lots of them, they will reach us soon," Thyra warned.

"I have a hiding place that I use. No one knows of it. So, we will be safe there," Ailsa informed them.

"What part of *we* involves *you*? You are not a Viking! You are not one of us!" snapped Revna, still not trusting Ailsa.

"Your suspicion and miss trust need to be directed towards your enemy. Now come, I am not your enemy," Ailsa snapped back, growing increasingly agitated with Revna.

"We are Vikings. We do not retreat, and I am not going anywhere without finding Toke."

"We need to make a decision fast," Thyra warned.

"Where is this hiding place?" Arne asked.

"It's a secret location; I've never shown it to anyone. It's big enough for all of us comfortably. I can take you there."

"No! Not without Toke," Revna insisted.

"Stop being so stubborn, Revna. We have a hostage. Let's follow her. Worst case, by the end of the night, we have two hostages," Ulf grinned.

"You will never find out what happened to your friend...."

"He is not just a friend," Revna snapped.

"If you die here, you will never find him," Ailsa said slowly.

"Leif?" Revna asked, "What is your command?"

"We go with Ailsa," Leif answered.

CHAPTER 9

OUTSIDE THE VILLAGE, close to the shoreline, the land jutted out into the water. And the land surrounding the rocky edge raised high up the cliff. This was the true Point; not the village below. High on the ridge sat the ruins of an old castle. It was considered haunted by the ghosts of the past, a rumour that became superstition. Ailsa was all too happy to allow people to believe such folklore. Walls lay in crumble, and rocks fell from the old towers when the winds grew too high. But to Ailsa, it was home.

Most of the building was ruined, save for the great hall, a few bedrooms, the dungeon below the keep, and part of the central tower. To the Vikings' surprise, it was a much shorter journey to safety, and they were grateful, as more British troops rode into the village to search them out. Like hounds seeking blood, they searched home after home with the hope of finding those who killed their men.

Arriving to the castle, Ailsa directed Leif, Ulf, and Arne to the dungeon where they could question their prisoner without creating a disturbance. It was a slow beginning. The men didn't speak much English, and the British commander didn't speak Danish. But Leif and the others would not let that stop them.

Thyra and Revna followed Ailsa to the lower part of the tower. They looked around in surprise and smiled at the home Ailsa had made from something that lay in ruin. Tapestries hung from the walls, and the furnishings all looked like they were made with the most excellent craftsmanship. It was cosy, intact, and spoke a lot about who Ailsa was.

"You have made this place a beautiful home," Revna said, stroking the edges of a tapestry of a white horse in a meadow.

"Thank you."

"I'd take it. She didn't warm up to me so fast," Thyra winked.

"Do you live here alone?" Revna asked.

"No, I live with my mother, Robyn."

Ailsa's mother walked in as if on cue, surprised to see Thyra and Revna. When Ailsa saw the panic in her eyes, she quickly explained the situation and Robyn softened. She was happy that Ailsa finally had some friends. Scurrying off to the kitchen, Robyn returned with a large pot of stew, glad to be doting on the women. Robyn was an excellent judge of character and seeing how she put Revna at ease, Ailsa relaxed a little.

"How did you both end up here?" Thyra asked as she enjoyed dipping bread into her stew.

Ailsa looked over to her mother, nodding that it was okay to talk. Robyn smiled, sitting opposite Revna and Thyra she sipped her drink before telling her story.

"Three and twenty years ago, I walked along the shore to find a beautiful, tall, and light-haired man. He had become shipwrecked. I brought him to my village and offered him a place to stay while he repaired his ship. It didn't take long for the ship to be repaired, but my Sven had stayed. He was a good man, and we fell hopelessly in love," Robyn spoke fondly, the love for her Viking still there in her eyes and in how she smiled saying his name.

"It was to my detriment that I should fall in love with such a good man. He was so kind, gentle, thoughtful, and brave. I assumed that all Vikings were like him. I had never met one before. But my village had a history with Vikings that I was unaware of; they cast me out for loving him."

"What did you do?" Thyra asked, enthralled by the story.

"I managed to convince them that Sven was different. When he left on what he said would be a short trip and never returned.... I found out I was with child. I was shamed, mocked, and cut off from my family. My family was thought of quite highly, so the rest of the village turned their back on me too," Robyn spoke, wiping a stray tear from her eye.

Even after all these years, it was still a subject that held so much pain. The wound cut deep, leaving a weeping scar that never seemed to heal.

"I had nowhere to go, so I took up residence here. I made money by doing odd jobs here and there, clothing repairs, herb collection, etc. I worked until I couldn't anymore. Then, I travelled to a neighbouring village to give birth to Ailsa and travelled back once I was able."

Ailsa walked around to her mother, wrapping her arms around her shoulders, and gently pressing a kiss to her forehead.

"When I was old enough, I did what I could to support us both. I saw travellers stealing from the market; that's when I knew. I became a thief."

"She never took more than what she felt was owed," Robyn spoke up as if she felt the need to defend her daughter's actions.

"Owed?" Revna asked.

"Was it not the village's responsibility to care for widows and orphans?" Ailsa replied.

"I suppose you are right," Revan said, returning to her food.

Robyn sighed heavily. But it was a sigh of longing, a sigh of remembering something with great fondness and love.

"My Sven, he was a beauty, you know. That is where my darling gets her eyes," Robyn mused, pinching Ailsa's chin and smiling up at her.

"The village shunned me because they had heard the stories of Viking raiders. But, no matter how much I told them that Sven was not like the others, they wouldn't even give him a chance. I see the same kindness and loyalty in you two," Robyn looked between Thyra and Revna.

"My Sven was not like those horrid Vikings my village feared and nothing like the monsters who carved the markings on the door."

Ailsa had been so lost in her mother's story about her father that she hadn't noticed Leif come in. She only became aware of his presence when he knocked into a chair. He was tired and frustrated, and from the way he eyed the pot in the middle of the table, he was hungry. She wondered how much of her mother's story he had heard.

CHAPTER 10

ULF, Arne, and Sven joined them in the room. Using Robyn's distraction of hurrying to serve up food, Leif ran around and grabbed Ailsa. He dragged her through the door and out into the hallway, his grip tightened, causing Ailsa to whine and claw at his hand.

"What was she talking about?" Leif demanded, shaking her arm, his nails digging into her skin.

"Do you always intend to be so rough with me?" she teased.

She had to admit, she was more than a little turned on by Leif's control of her, or was it just Leif in general?

"The markings? Where are they?" Leif demanded, ignoring her comment.

"It's just some scratchings on the door. I'm surprised you didn't see them when we arrived. They are quite deeply embedded in the wood."

"Show me," Leif ordered.

Walking through the hall and down a small set of stairs towards the great hall, she showed him the markings. They had been carved on the door to the great hall and the door at the main entrance to the castle. Both markings were identical; he ran his fingers over the markings. His pulse raced. This was the lead they had been looking for.

"They are runes. They say a name...."

"What name?" Ailsa asked.

"Halfden," Leif growled low.

Anticipation, longing, and frustration ran through Leif. Then, without thinking, in a frenzy, he grabbed Ailsa by the shoulders, shaking her a bit forcefully.

"Did they leave something?"

"Leif, you are crazed, and you're hurting me," Ailsa complained.

He released his grip but not the mad look in his eyes.

"Did they bury something?"

Ailsa took a step back, shocked. She gasped, "How did you know?"

"They did. *Where!?*"

"The night they arrived and we were forced to serve them. They said that they would kill my mother and me if we didn't. I only avoided being raped by keeping a large carving knife tucked in my clothes. But, yes, when they thought I was sleeping, I heard something in the great hall."

"Did you see anything?"

"No one knows these halls as I do. I crept out and watched them from one of the broken towers above. When they eventually left, I tried to dig it up, but the stone was too heavy."

The Jarl's hoard was here after all. Everything had worked out. Leif allowed himself to feel the rush of success for the first time since arriving on these shores.

"Where?" He was softening to her again.

"The great hall. Under the hearthstone. Truth be told, I was too scared to look. They said they would be back.... Leif....Leif," Ailsa called after him as he raced past her to the great hall.

Ulf, Sven, and Arne had ventured out searching for Leif. The commander had tried to escape and had received a rather nasty break to his nose when Revna planted a punch square in his face.

"Leif, what should we do with him? Leif.... Leif.... where is he going?" Sven asked, dragging the prisoner behind him.

Ailsa and the men raced to keep up with Leif. Watching from the door, Ulf and Arne both tried to find out what was wrong, but Leif ignored every question. Instead, he searched the hearth for any stone that looked to be recently overturned. A large square slab was in the centre of the floor directly in front of the hearth. Scratch marks lay deep at its edges, and dust and dirt scattered around it.

"This is it," Leif whispered. "Ulf, Arne, help me with this," he ordered.

Pulling his sword from his belt, he jammed it into the gap between stones, using it to put enough pressure underneath to lift the stone for the others to grab. Together they pried up the stone, tossing it aside, cracking it down the centre. Under the stone sat a large wooden chest with the Jarl's markings carved into the top.

Pulling it from the hole, they quickly tore off the lid. It was the money that they had been searching for. Gold glistened against the light of the fireplace. Everyone gasped in surprise.

"I can't believe it," Sven breathed.

"We finally found it," Ulf cheered.

Suddenly, the British commander struggled against Sven's grip, but Sven held tight. The commander began to shout – in Danish – to the surprise of everyone in the room.

"What did he say?" Leif snarled.

"It's mine! I was assigned to find it! It's mine!" the commander roared.

"Well, look at that. You do speak Danish after all," Revna snarled, popping into the great hall after following all the noise.

CHAPTER 11

REVNA SQUARED up to the commander. With the money found, they had no more use for their prisoner. Or so they led him to believe.

"Now we have found the Jarl's hoard, can I kill him?" Revna snarled.

"I see no reason to keep him around," Leif replied.

Revna pulled a blade from her belt, holding it to the man's throat.

"Wait! Wait! I can help you find your friend!" He spat, panicked.

"Talk! Before my sister cuts out your tongue," Sven shook the man by the shoulders.

"We spotted you and him outside the inn. We assumed that he was one of the Jarl's men. When my men knocked you out, we took him."

"We worked that out already," Revna snapped.

"Why did you take him?" Ailsa asked.

The commander looked back at her, confused, "Why else? So he could lead us to the gold."

The group erupted into laughter, a laughter that filled the room and made Ailsa smile. It was the first time the Vikings had shown any emotion other than anger. She felt her heart flutter seeing Leif's eyes crinkle. His smile was wide and bright, and she wanted to see more of it. While his grim, brooding side was very attractive to her, she found that she liked this softer side just as much.

"You took the wrong man," Sven chuckled.

"Toke will have taken your men on a wild goose chase all night just for the fun of it," Revna said, tucking her blade back into her belt. "Sven, Thyra, are you coming to find Toke with me?"

"Sure am. I can't wait to hear what he has been up to all night," Sven smiled, wiping a stray tear from the corner of his eye, as a result of laughing so hard.

Sven handed the commander over to Ulf and Arne, leaving Leif to count the gold. Ailsa took this as her sign to leave the men in peace, heading back to the tower to finish dining with her mother. After she helped her mother clean up after dinner, she heard the others returning. Heading to the window, she watched as Revna, Sven, and Thyra returned with an even larger-looking man than Leif. They were smiling and laughing. And it warmed her heart. Dashing back to the great hall, she was pleased to see that Leif was still there. The commander had been tied to a chain and was guarded closely by Arne lest he tried to escape again.

"Toke, brother! I was worried I would never see your ugly face again," Ulf joked, slapping Toke hard on the shoulder before pulling him into a tight hug.

"Going to take more than the British to send me to Valhalla, my friend," Toke replied.

"How did you find him?" Leif asked, embracing his comrade.

"We asked ourselves, where is the stupidest place to search for gold? So, we headed to the shore, and on our way there, Toke found us," Revna answered, clinging to Toke's side like a devoted puppy dog.

"When I realised they thought I worked with the Jarl, I had them looking in underwater caves for sunken treasure," Toke said, stopping abruptly when his eyes clasped on the British commander. "I decided to take a page out of their book. I set a trap. Your men underestimated me. I am a Viking. I was born to the sea. I drowned twelve of your men."

The commander sat back and swallowed hard as Toke towered over him.

"Glad to see you can swim better than that day in the caves," Sven joked.

"That was a fluke. I swim like a fish. I was quite enjoying myself; I need to swim more often. Travelling by land is no fun; I miss the waves," Toke said, heading back to Revna's side and wrapping her in his embrace.

"So, what does this mean for him?" Ailsa asked, pointing to the British commander.

"You will take back a message," Leif grinned, "You will tell your leader that the Jarl's gold left these shores with him. There is no coin for you; there shall be no war."

Revna stepped forward, wrapping an arm around Ailsa's shoulders.

"We will know if the message is not delivered as per our instruction. You see this one? She is the best assassin you have ever seen. She can move with the shadows; you will never see her coming. If you do not deliver the message word for word, she will slit your throat while you sleep," Revna winked at Ailsa.

Ailsa was pleased that Revna had appeared to trust her finally. While she had never had an affliction for blood lust or ever thought of hurting anyone, the idea of having Revna's skills brought out goose-bumps. The commander swallowed hard, nodding his head vigorously in agreement.

"Say you understand," Ailsa spoke up, caught up in the moment.

Leif suppressed a chuckle, standing firm.

"I understand.... word for word....no war," he stuttered.

With a nod from Leif, Arne untied the commander; as soon as he rose to his feet, the commander bolted out of the castle, not once looking back.

"I can't believe we found it. Our mission is complete," Sven grinned, causing the group to erupt into cheer.

All seemed settled. They had accomplished their mission. Robyn, hearing the cheers, came into the great hall carrying a small barrel of mead. Ailsa ran to help her as celebrations began. The expedition had been a complete success. The gods had answered Leif's prayers, except Leif still had one loose end he wanted to take care of before he sailed back to the King.

CHAPTER 12

EVERYONE WAS DISTRACTED by celebrations that no one noticed Ailsa slip out of the great hall. No one that is, except for Leif. Leaving his men behind, he slipped from the room and followed Ailsa down the halls. She hesitated by her door; Leif used that moment to capture her one last time. Grabbing her and spinning her around, trapping her between the door and him.

"You know, I could hear you following me? You are terrible at this," Ailsa grinned.

Leif clasped her hands together and raised them above her head.

"If I'm so terrible, why do you always end up in my arms?" Leif growled, running his nose along her jaw, letting his lips trail kisses down her neck.

"Maybe I like being in your arms," Ailsa whispered.

"I think you like danger," Leif whispered, nibbling at her earlobe.

"Maybe I like dangerous men."

"I am a very dangerous man," Leif responded.

"Despite what you may think, I'm a very dangerous woman."

"I don't doubt it for a second," Leif growled.

Ailsa hooked her leg through Leif's and pulled her hands free. With one slick movement, she had flipped their positions. He was now the one trapped by her. Leif chuckled deep in the back of his throat.

"Okay, now you have me. What do you intend to do with me?"

Keeping her eyes locked on his, she opened the door and pushed him inside. The room was small; a few stumbled steps, and Leif crashed onto the bed. Ailsa turned to close the door. Leif lept from the bed, pinning her against the wall.

"Do you always intend to be so rough with me?" Ailsa teased.

Leif stepped back, nervous he had upset or hurt Ailsa. She spun around with a mischievous grin and a glint in her eyes.

"Did I tell you to stop?"

Taking the hint, Leif grabbed her and pulled her to him, planting a kiss of building passion and all of his pent-up lust. Ailsa shrugged out of his hold, wrapping her arms around his neck, grabbing fistfuls of Leif's long, thick curls. Pulling him closer, Ailsa kissed him back, their tongues exploring in a wild array of arousal.

Leif ran his hands down Ailsa's shoulders, gripping the top of her dress and ripping it open. Pinning Ailsa against the wall, she wrapped a leg around his hip as he trailed his lips down her neck, taking one of her breasts in his mouth. Then, holding her up with one hand, he slipped his other hand under her skirt, pulling it up and running his fingers between her thighs. Ailsa rested her head back and moaned deeply, craving more of his touch.

Her sweetness coated Leif's fingers; he loved how her body responded to him. Dropping her skirt, she watched as he brought his fingers to his lips, wrapping his tongue around them, tasting her. It caused Ailsa's breath to quicken, and she felt her arousal stirring. She wanted him; she needed him inside her.

Pushing him back, she tore at his clothes, but she was not as strong as he. Smiling back at her, he made quick work of stripping while Ailsa worked to remove the torn remains of her dress. Ailsa knew that Leif was a strong man, built of muscle. But she gasped seeing him bare in front of her. Gently running her hands over his chest, down his stomach, letting her fingers trace his abs before wrapping her fingers around the thick bulging muscle between his legs.

Leif sucked in a gasp of air; he had craved her touch ever since they met. Stroking him, she kissed him passionately until Leif couldn't take much more. Then, scooping her up into his arms, he carried her the few steps to the bed. Laying her down, Leif climbed on top of her, his hands roaming over every inch of her as his mouth trailed closely behind. Ailsa moaned under his touch.

Each kiss and teasing caress drove Ailsa insane, "Leif...."

"You have teased me since we met; now it's my turn," Leif groaned as he pushed her thighs apart. Ailsa entangled her fingers in his hair, holding him in place. He spread her apart and teased the aching bud between her legs with the tip of his tongue. Ailsa cried out as her pleasure built. His mouth not leaving her, reaching up, he pawed at her breasts, tweaking her nipples.

He loved how she tasted; he sucked her into his mouth, lapping her up. Ailsa arched her back and moaned his name, pulling his hair until it hurt. Leif moved back, letting her pleasure ease, climbing up her with trailing kisses from her hip to her breasts before letting her taste herself on his tongue.

Ailsa wrapped her legs around his waist; she didn't want to let him go.

"Leif, I need you; I need more...."

Leif grinned down at her. The pleasure of watching her writhe in ecstasy under his teasing touch only made him ache more. Slowly, he pushed himself inside her, gasping at how good she felt tight around him. He started making love to her slowly until she was close, begging for more. Clenching herself tightly around him, she wrapped her arms around his neck, pulling him closer to her. Biting his ear hard enough to make him groan, she growled seductively in his ear, "Leif, I need you to ride me."

"Say it again," Leif growled.

"I need you to ride me.... Hard."

"You want it rough?" Leif growled.

"Yes," Ailsa moaned.

He untangled himself from Ailsa's grasp in one swift movement, flipping her over. Having her on all fours in front of him, her beautifully round buttocks were almost too much for him to take.

"Head down, arch your back."

As Ailsa got in position, Leif spread her cheeks and pleased her with his tongue once again. Ailsa moaned in ecstasy; he was more skilled than anyone she had been with before.

"Leif!" Ailsa yelled.

Gripping her hips, he slammed into her, stretching her as she clenched around him. He made love to her in long, hard strokes, wrapping her hair around his hand, forcing her to arch her back more, giving him room to push a little deeper.

It wasn't long before Ailsa came apart around him. Leif spanked Ailsa's buttock, pounding her harder. It wasn't long before her body was wracked with another mind-shattering explosion of pleasure. She screamed his name until he, too, felt his pleasure take hold.

They fell apart together, crumbling to the bed, panting. Their sweat-glistened bodies wrapped around each other like two pieces of a puzzle meant to be together. Leif wrapped his arm around Ailsa, pulling her close, kissing her gently on the forehead. She rested her head on his chest, listening to the rapid beat of his heart. It was a lullaby that lulled her to sleep.

They woke hours later, still lovingly wrapped in each other's arms. But Ailsa had aching in her heart, questions she wanted to ask but was too scared of the answers.

"Something on your mind?" Leif asked sleepily, placing a kiss on her forehead.

"I was just thinking how good it feels to be here, in your arms."

"You're scared I'm going to leave?"

Ailsa said nothing as if speaking her answer would make it real.

Leif leant up on one arm, cupping her face and stroking her chin with his thumb.

"It took me a lifetime to find you. I believe my mission was not to find the King's gold but to find you. I promise I will not leave as your father did to your mother. I will take you everywhere I go.... you and your mother."

Ailsa was speechless.

"My little thief, you have stolen my heart. And I am going to spend the rest of my time trying to steal yours."

"It's already yours," she whispered back.

Climbing on top of him and kissing him deeply, they made love, over and over, until the sun rose and set.

EPILOGUE

LEIF KEPT his promise when he travelled back to Denmark to report his success to the King. He had taken Ailsa and Robyn with him. The King had been so pleased with their help on the mission that he gave Ailsa and her mother a sizable reward.

"I declare a new settlement be erected at the Point. Leif, you will be in charge of the settlement. I do not need to tell you what a huge honour this is," declared the King.

"It is my honour to serve you, my King," Leif said, bending his knee, overjoyed the King would trust him with such an honour.

"Your task is to help keep the peace. I do not like the growing dissent, and a war between our lands is the last thing we need. You will need someone who knows the lands to help you. Ailsa, please step forward."

Nervously, Ailsa and her mother joined Leif, bowing their heads to the King.

"Do you accept the honour of ruling the new settlement by Leif's side?" the King asked.

She looked to Lief who offered a knowing wink and a cheeky grin.

"It would be my honour," Ailsa beamed.

Happy with the turn of events, the King arranged a feast in the group's honour. Ulf seemed to have finally made amends with his father, who proudly boasted of his son's involvement in the mission. As the night drew on, the group gathered one last time.

"We did it, brothers," Leif cheered.

Revna coughed, covering a slur.

"And sisters," Leif raised his cup.

"What will you all do now?" Ailsa asked.

Giving in a moment's contemplation, Ulf and Arne grinned, "We will accompany you back to the new settlement. If you will have us? Bodil and Coline call those lands their home, and we couldn't ask them to leave," Ulf grinned.

Leif offered Ulf and Arne a hand, shaking them both hard, "I would be honoured."

"You all know of our plans," Sven smiled weakly.

"Have you asked Thyra what she wants to do? The Scottish settlement has always been her home, the sword maidens were her life," worried Reva.

"Not yet, I'm...."

"You need not worry. Thyra loves you. The settlement isn't going anywhere," Ailsa reassured him.

"You have picked a good one there, Leif," Sven winked.

"The best," Leif answered, pulling Ailsa to his side.

BACK AT THE POINT, Leif and Ailsa began to rebuild their castle. The village was not happy with a new Viking settlement being erected so close to their homes, but with Robyn and Ailsa's help, it wasn't long before peace shone on the horizon. All was finally looking well.

"It is time, brother," Sven said.

At the shoreline lay a large ship. Revna and Toke prepared to sail.

"I can't believe you are finally getting your dream. You deserve this, brother. You all deserve this," Leif grinned, shaking Sven's hand.

Revna and Toke joined them on the shore as Arne, Ulf, Bodil, And Coline joined them.

"This is it, this is the end," Ulf said, pain in his voice.

"Not the end. A new beginning. We will see each other again.

Family always finds a way back to each other," Revna said as tears glistened in her eyes.

"Revna, dare I say you have gotten soft since you found love?" Arne teased.

"Believe me, brother; she has not," Toke laughed.

The group said their goodbyes and watched as Sven, Thyra, Revna, and Toke sailed off into the horizon.

"I'm happy for them," Bodil said.

"I'm happy for us," Ailsa smiled.

"Right, that's enough sadness for one day. Come, we have work to do. This settlement isn't going to raise itself," Leif ordered.

THE END
Did you enjoy The King's Raiders?
Please consider reviewing it on <u>Goodreads</u>, <u>Bookbub</u> or your favorite retailer. Reviews help me reach new readers.

Read The Viking Settlers, the next book in the Hot Vikings series. For updates on book releases, book recommendations, Viking Trivia, Sales, and GIVEAWAYS, subscribe to my Newsletter!
www.peytonlawsonromance.com